Main Street

Coming Apart

Ann M. Martin

SCHOLASTIC INC.

NEW YORK ◇ TORONTO ◇ LONDON ◇ AUCKLAND
SYDNEY ◇ MEXICO CITY ◇ NEW DELHI ◇ HONG KONG

ISBN 978-0-545-06896-3

12 11 10 9 8 7 6 5 4 3 2 1   10 11 12 13 14 15/0

Printed in the U.S.A.   23

First printing, September 2010

Camden Falls

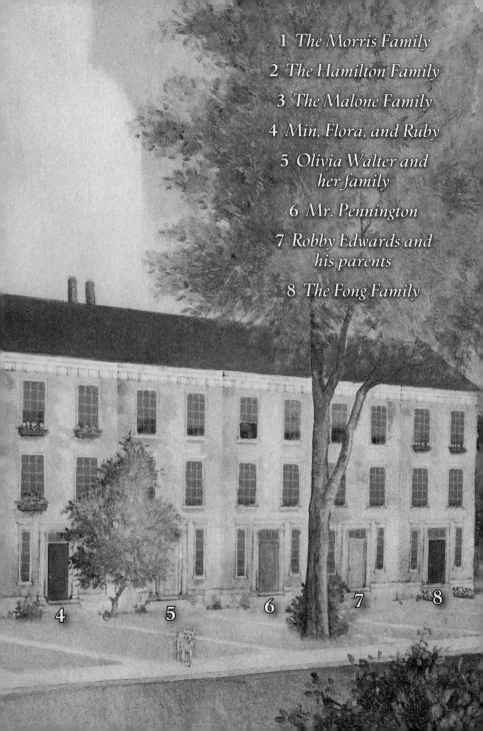

1 *The Morris Family*

2 *The Hamilton Family*

3 *The Malone Family*

4 *Min, Flora, and Ruby*

5 *Olivia Walter and her family*

6 *Mr. Pennington*

7 *Robby Edwards and his parents*

8 *The Fong Family*

4 5 6 7 8

CHAPTER I

Back to School

"Are you going to eat that?"

Nikki Sherman looked up from her plate, which held a slice of unbuttered bread and part of a carrot, to the boy who was sitting across the cafeteria table from her. She assumed Jacob was referring to the bread and not the carrot tip. "No," she replied. "Do you want it?"

Jacob held out his hand. "Thanks."

Although Nikki liked Jacob very much, she thought privately that he was something of a human Dustbuster, although she would never have said as much to Olivia Walter, who was one of her best friends — and Jacob's girlfriend. Nikki passed Jacob the bread. "It has a little tomato sauce on it," she said.

Jacob waved one hand in the air, his way of saying he couldn't care less, and used his other hand to stuff the bread in his mouth in one enormous bite. Nikki would have been horrified, except that she had an eighteen-year-old brother, and she was used to watching him eat. When he was Jacob's age, he could put away three or four helpings of dinner, followed by two helpings of dessert, followed by a bedtime snack of three whole English muffins with peanut butter (translation: six slices). So she wasn't surprised that Jacob wanted her bread after having finished a rather large lunch. But she still couldn't get the Dustbuster image out of her head.

Jacob swallowed the bread, and Nikki saw him looking around the cafeteria. His eyes fell on one of the food lines. Was he seriously considering buying something else to eat? He had cleaned his plate and everyone else's at the table. The lunches at Camden Falls Central High School were pretty good, but still.

Not that Nikki had anything to compare them to except the lunches at Camden Falls Elementary, where she had gone to school until this year. Now Nikki and her friends were seventh-graders at the big central school in Camden Falls, Massachusetts. Switching schools was just one of many changes they had faced lately.

Jacob scarfed up the lone carrot tip while Flora, Nikki's other best friend, twirled an apple around by its stem. She gave the apple a vigorous spin, then leaned over and whispered to Nikki, "If Tanya and Melody don't stop staring at us, their eyes are going to bug out of their sockets."

"They're not staring at *us*, you know," Nikki whispered back.

"Okay, at Olivia and Jacob, but it's the same thing. They keep staring over here. They're making me nervous."

"Just ignore them. Pretend they're mosquitoes."

"I can't. It's more like they're vultures, and it's really hard to ignore vultures."

Nikki sneaked a look at the next table, where Tanya Rhodes and Melody Becker were sitting side by side, each burdened by several pounds of silver jewelry and each sporting a newly colored streak in her hair — pink for Tanya, green for Melody. Their eyes were trained on Jacob and Olivia.

"They *are* kind of vulturelike," agreed Nikki, forgetting to whisper.

"What?" said Olivia from across the table.

Nikki blushed. "Nothing. I'll tell you later."

Olivia swallowed a mouthful of pasta. "So, Nikki, when is your dad coming?"

Nikki could feel her blush deepen. She shrugged. The only problem with the fact that Jacob rarely left Olivia's side was that the three girls had almost no time to themselves anymore, especially when they were in school. Nikki was glad that Olivia had been singled out by Jacob to be his girlfriend, but there was no way Nikki was going to talk about her family in front of him. She considered Olivia and Flora her sisters. She did not consider Jacob her brother.

"Your dad hasn't decided yet?" Olivia tried again.

"You know, I'm kind of glad to be back in school," was Nikki's answer. "Christmas was fun and everything, but it's nice to be in our old routine. Plus, I get to see you guys every day."

Olivia frowned. "Nikki, I asked if your dad —"

Olivia levitated out of her seat then, and Nikki suspected that Flora had kicked her under the table.

"Ow," said Olivia, reaching down to rub her shin.

It was a Friday in January and the end of the first week of school after the holiday break. Nikki truly had enjoyed her vacation, but she was also truly glad to be back at school. Of all the changes facing her and her friends, the biggest one, in Nikki's opinion, was her own parents' impending divorce and her father's return to Camden Falls to finalize things. It was all making Nikki very anxious, and she was grateful to be able to escape to school.

Her father had been gone for over a year now, one blissful year in which her fractured family had slowly been able to mend without him. It was as if her family had been a broken vase, and once the vase had been glued back together, it turned out there was an extra piece that didn't belong. Her father.

When Mr. Sherman had walked out their door the November before last, following an autumn of fights and threats and arguments, of punches ducked and kicks sidestepped, Nikki had breathed a sigh of relief.

She hadn't cared that despite her father's promises to send money, her mother was going to have to support Nikki and her brother and sister all by herself. She hadn't cared about living far out in the country without Mr. Sherman for protection. Tobias, her brother, would take over that role. There had been nothing at all that Nikki would miss. Not unless she planned to miss the sight of her father staggering to the bathroom in his pajamas at three o'clock in the afternoon, or the sound of the phone ringing when his current boss called to say that Mr. Sherman had missed work three days in a row, or the quiet of the house when the phone *didn't* ring because her father had spent the phone bill money at the bar over in Essex and their service had been turned off again.

Mr. Sherman had come back briefly that Christmas, but for months after he'd left the second time, Nikki had lived in blissful ignorance, thinking she would never see her father again. How could she have thought that? Of course he was going to have to return, at least temporarily. Her mother wanted a divorce from him, and her father wanted some of the things he had left behind in their house — the rest of his clothes, everything that was his that he hadn't jammed into his suitcase on that November day.

And now he was planning his trip back to Camden Falls, and Nikki, as much as she wanted to get things over with, was as nervous as the stray dogs that hung

♡ 5 ♡

around her property, the ones that had so enraged her father. Her mother was nervous, too, she knew, even though she did a good job of hiding it. Mae, who was seven, was nervous — that was obvious — and Tobias was so nervous that he planned to take a break from his freshman year at college so he could be at home until Mr. Sherman had packed up and was gone for good. Tobias refused to leave his mother and sisters alone with his father. He wasn't sure how he would make up the coursework he'd miss, but knew he would straighten things out eventually.

Nikki let her eyes wander to the cafeteria windows and beyond, to the school lawn, brown now in a winter that so far had yielded very little snow. In her mind, she continued her journey along the tree-lined lanes that led to Main Street, to the shops and businesses that were the heart of town. This part of town, though, was not Nikki's Camden Falls. Hers lay several miles away in fields and woods, where deer outnumbered people and where at night the only light came from the moon and the windows of her own house. Main Street was Flora's Camden Falls, and Olivia's. Nikki's friends were comfortable strolling along the sidewalk, greeting shopkeepers and visiting their families' stores. Needle and Thread, the sewing store, was owned and run by Flora's and Olivia's grandmothers, and Sincerely Yours, a new gift-basket store, belonged to Olivia's parents. The girls were as at home on Main

Street as they were on nearby Aiken Avenue, where Flora lived with her younger sister, Ruby, and her grandmother Min, and where Olivia lived with her little brothers and her parents.

It was funny, Nikki thought, that Flora felt so comfortable on Main Street, while Nikki sometimes still felt like an outsider there. After all, Nikki had grown up in Camden Falls, while Flora and Ruby had arrived less than two years earlier. But the sisters had been plunked into life on Main Street and Aiken Avenue, with its large cast of store owners and neighbors, while Nikki had grown up in her isolated house in the country.

Nikki dragged her mind back to the cafeteria just as Jacob stood up, fished in his pocket for his swipe card, and said, "Anybody want anything else?"

Nikki, Olivia, and Flora shook their heads, and Jacob shrugged, as if he couldn't believe the girls weren't still hungry. As soon as he was out of earshot, Olivia screeched, "Flora! Why did you kick me?"

"Because Nikki doesn't want to talk about her father, not here in front of Jacob . . . and anyone else who might be listening," she added, casting her eyes in the direction of the jewelry-laden vultures.

"Sor-ry," said Olivia. But then she added, "Actually, it would be nice if we could sit by ourselves sometimes, just the three of us, so we could talk." She paused. "I mean, really talk."

"Is there something you want to talk about, too?" asked Nikki curiously. "Something you can't say in front of Jacob?"

"Well," Olivia started to reply, then glanced up and whispered, "Never mind. Jacob's paying already." A few moments later, Jacob slid into his chair again, this time carrying a piece of chocolate cake wrapped in cellophane. The cake disappeared in three mouthfuls.

"Hey, you guys," said Flora, smiling suddenly. "You have to come see Janie again soon. She is *so* cute. And you can practically watch her grow. I know she's only been here a few weeks, but already she's completely different. She smiles now, and I know it isn't just gas, no matter what Aunt Allie says."

"Oh!" exclaimed Olivia. "You know what I saw in Bubble Gum the other day? Little baby hair bows. You should get one for her, Flora."

"That's perfect. I'm making her a pair of polka-dotted overalls. I could buy a bow to go with them."

At the mere mention of Janie, Flora's new little cousin, Jacob's eyes glazed over. This was the one change in the lives of Nikki and her friends that the girls could actually talk about in front of Jacob — and he wasn't interested in it. Well, that wasn't entirely fair, Nikki reflected. Jacob had been happy for Flora's aunt Allie when she had adopted Janie, but talk of baby clothes and chubby arms and hair bows and night-lights and crib bumpers, and especially dirty diapers and spit-up, caused Jacob to tune out and go off into some unrelated twelve-year-old-boy world.

"Aunt Allie just can't figure out Janie's sleep patterns," Flora was saying. "Three nights in a row Janie slept for six hours straight, but then last night she was up every two hours —"

Flora was interrupted by Jacob, who suddenly announced, "Did you guys hear that the community center might have to close two days a week?"

"What?" said Nikki, whose mind had been snugly in Janie's bedroom. "Seriously?"

"Yup." Jacob wiped a nearly invisible dot of frosting off of the cellophane and licked it from his finger. "It's expensive to keep it open every day. Not as many people can afford to take classes now, so my mom said the people who run it are going to have to let some of the employees go and cut some of the classes and programs."

"That's horrible!" exclaimed Olivia. "I took an art class there once. And Mom and Dad were going to sign my brothers up for basketball."

"Mae's been begging to take ballet," said Nikki. "Mom was going to save up for the summer classes for her. I wonder if ballet will be cut."

"*I* wonder if anything is going to have to close down completely," said Olivia darkly. "I know Mom and Dad are worried about Sincerely Yours. And if they're worried, I'll bet other people are worried about their stores.

And their jobs. You know, Mary Louise Detwiler's mom lost her job, and then her dad lost his job, too."

"Oh," said Nikki faintly, and her eyes strayed to the end of the next table, where Mary Louise was sitting, attempting to read a book in the midst of the noise and commotion.

"Min said business at the store has been really slow lately," spoke up Flora. "But Needle and Thread has been around for years. I think Min and Gigi can keep it going."

"Hulit's is closing," said Jacob.

"What!" exclaimed Olivia. "The shoe store? Where are we supposed to buy shoes?"

"At the mall, I guess," said Nikki, trying to sound casual. But an insistent and very annoying voice in her head was whispering, What if Mom's job gets cut? Then what happens to us? Nikki tried to will the voice away and only succeeded when lunch ended and it was time for her next class.

"See you guys!" Jacob said to Nikki and Flora as he stood up from the table.

Nikki looked expectantly at Olivia, who, she was sure, wanted to say something in private to her friends, but Olivia merely smiled tightly and followed Jacob into the corridor.

"Is something going on with Olivia?" Nikki asked Flora.

Flora shrugged. "We didn't see each other that much over vacation."

"Huh," said Nikki. This was surprising, considering Flora and Olivia lived next door to each other.

"Yeah, huh," said Flora. "She and Jacob were always together."

Nikki knew that her mother had arranged for Mae to attend the Camden Falls Elementary after-school program precisely so that Nikki wouldn't have to be responsible for her little sister every afternoon. And on those days when Nikki had plans with Olivia and Flora, she truly appreciated the arrangement. But on days like today, when the school bus dropped her off at the end of her lane and she walked to her house alone, she missed Mae's company. Sometimes the house felt creepy, even when Paw-Paw glued himself to Nikki's side.

Nikki unlocked her front door, talking to Paw-Paw as she did so. "I'm home, boy. You can come out now. Go play in the yard for a while." And Paw-Paw, the big brown stray, endlessly patient, who had become a member of Nikki's family only after her father had left, bolted onto the porch and into the yard, where he ran around and around like a cartoon dog. Nikki half expected to see a circular rut form under his speeding paws.

Nikki dumped her school things by the front door, made a snack, and gave a bite of it to Paw-Paw. Then she settled at the kitchen table to start her homework. She could work at the desk in her room, but she felt vulnerable up there, so far from the front door. In the kitchen, she had a view of the driveway — and an escape route. She wasn't sure what she was afraid of, exactly. But she didn't relish being the only one at home on these silent, dark winter afternoons.

When at long last she saw the headlights of her mother's car in their lane, she let out her breath and closed her books.

"They're here," she said to Paw-Paw. "Mom and Mae are home."

Paw-Paw ran full tilt toward the front door, which was only four feet away, so he nearly crashed into it.

Nikki laughed. "Klutz," she said, and wrapped her arms around him before opening the door.

"Hi! I'm home!" Mae announced, squeezing past Nikki and Paw-Paw, her arms laden with library books, art projects, and stray articles of clothing. On her head she wore a hat made of balloons. "Like it?" she asked Nikki.

"It's stunning," Nikki replied, and grinned at her mother. "I started dinner," she added.

Mrs. Sherman heaved a sigh and kicked off her shoes. "You're an angel," she said.

"Am I an angel?" asked Mae.

"Most of the time," Mrs. Sherman replied.

Half an hour later, Nikki, Mae, and their mother were seated at the kitchen table, which was set for three, and Nikki was privately recalling the days when the table had been set for five. When her father was still at home, and Tobias was still in high school. When trouble could erupt at any moment between her father and her mother, between her father and Tobias. (Her father was always involved.) And trouble could lead to flying furniture and broken dishes and the need to run for cover.

As if Mae could read Nikki's thoughts, she now said, "Mommy? When is —" She paused. "When is your husband coming back?" Nikki would have laughed if she hadn't known what lay behind Mae's refusal to call her father Daddy.

"A week from tomorrow," Mrs. Sherman replied.

Mae nodded soberly. "And when is Tobias coming home?"

"A week from today."

"Yes!" Mae cried. She adjusted her balloon hat. "Maybe I'll make a hat like this for Tobias next week." She ate a bite of chicken, then said casually, "Tell me again why your husband is coming here."

"A few reasons," said Mrs. Sherman evenly. "First of all, he wants to see you and Nikki and Tobias. He hasn't seen you in a long time."

Mae made no comment.

"Also, he needs to finish moving out of the house. We talked about that. Do you remember what I said?"

Mae nodded.

"He's going to pack up the rest of his clothes and things so that he can take them to his new home."

"In South Carolina?" asked Mae.

"Yes. And then there's the divorce," said Mrs. Sherman. "We need to finish things up."

Nikki knew that her parents' divorce proceedings had already begun and that a lot had been accomplished long-distance, via mail. But now certain matters (her mother had been vague about just what these matters were) needed to be finalized in person with lawyers. And then her father would leave and, Nikki fervently hoped, be out of their lives for good.

"And when you're divorced, what will I be?" Mae asked her mother.

"What do you mean?"

"Will I be an orphan?"

Mrs. Sherman smiled. "No. You will still be Mae Sherman, my daughter and your father's daughter and Nikki and Tobias's sister. Okay?"

"Okay. What's for dessert?"

"Ice cream," Nikki replied.

"Goody." Mae turned her attention to Paw-Paw, who was begging silently but effectively by resting his great head on her knee and gazing into her eyes. "I'll sneak you a bite," Mae whispered, and the subject of her father was temporarily forgotten.

CHAPTER 2

Jane Marie

On Saturday morning, it was Flora's responsibility to take Daisy Dear on her pre-breakfast walk. Daisy was Min's golden retriever. The first time Flora had met the galumphing dog, she'd expected her to be fearless due to her large size. Instead, Daisy had turned out to be an enormous, well, scaredy-cat. She was afraid of cats, as a matter of fact. Only now, a year and a half after Flora and Ruby and King Comma, their own cat, had moved into their grandmother Min's house, could Daisy approach King with her tail wagging and her head held high. Nevertheless, Daisy shuddered at thunder and also had once fled upstairs when Min — Min! — had walked into the kitchen wearing an unfamiliar hat.

Flora ran down her front walk, pulled along exuberantly by Daisy and still tugging on her mittens as they went. The morning was chilly but not January chilly. It felt more like a morning in early November, with a promise of milder air later in the day.

"Are we ever going to get a snowstorm?" Flora asked Daisy. "I mean, a true snowstorm, when school closes and everything?"

Daisy glanced over her shoulder at Flora, as if to say that she really couldn't be bothered to have a conversation at that moment, and then made a fast left-hand turn onto the sidewalk and continued down Aiken Avenue in a big rush.

"Good morning, Flora!" called a cheerful voice.

Rudy Pennington, who lived two doors from Flora in the Row Houses, was ambling along his own front walk with Jacques, his ancient cocker spaniel, at the end of a tired-looking red leash. Jacques needed a lot of coaxing to keep moving, and Flora saw that despite Mr. Pennington's jolly words, his face was grave.

"Come on, old boy," he said softly.

Jacques stopped moving altogether and stared at Mr. Pennington.

"Is he all right?" asked Flora as Daisy, who loved Mr. Pennington and Jacques, turned up their walk and greeted them with a yip and a playful lunge.

"He's . . . I don't think he's feeling very well this morning." Mr. Pennington gave the leash a little tug and Jacques resumed his stiff walk to the curb.

"I'm sorry," said Flora. She was about to ask whether Mr. Pennington was going to take Jacques to the vet when the door in the next to the last house in the row opened and Robby Edwards leaned out, still wearing his pajamas.

"Good morning, Flora! Good morning, Mr. Pennington!" he called, in what Flora personally thought was rather a loud voice for such an early hour. "Mr. Pennington, is something wrong with Jacques?"

Robby, who was eighteen years old and had Down syndrome, was halfway out his door when Flora heard his father call him back inside.

"I hope he's not sick!" said Robby before he disappeared through his front door.

This was one of the very few things that Flora disliked about the Row Houses: Everyone knew everyone else's business. It was almost impossible not to. The old Row Houses, built in the 1800s, were actually one sprawling stone building divided into eight nearly identical attached homes. Although each home was a healthy size, so that the families had plenty of space, Flora sometimes felt that she and her neighbors were crowded on top of one another, everyone (Flora included) freely asking who was sick, how a school play had gone, whether a baby was teething yet, how business was doing.

When Flora and Ruby had moved to Camden Falls to live with Min, all the neighborliness had taken a bit of getting used to. On the one hand, Flora was grateful for it. She and her sister had lost their parents in a car accident a few months before the move, and Flora had still felt lost and somewhat rudderless on the June day when Min had driven her and Ruby and King Comma to their new home. The neighbors had welcomed them warmly and had swarmed in and out of Min's house, helping to unload the U-Haul and settle the girls in their new rooms. That had been nice, if overwhelming. But there were times when Flora wished for a bit more privacy, wished to be an anonymous twelve-year-old living under only Min's watchful eyes instead of the eyes of every adult in the Row Houses.

Still, it was fascinating to think that so many people lived under one roof. Flora stood back now and regarded the Row Houses. Starting at the left end there were the Morrises, the Hamiltons, and the Malones, then Min's house, Olivia's, Mr. Pennington's, and Robby's, and finally at the right end, the Fongs'. Twenty-eight people of a variety of races and backgrounds, ranging in age from Grace Fong, who was a baby, to Mr. Pennington, who was in his eighties. Plus several cats and dogs and Olivia's guinea pig, Sandy. Actually, thought Flora, who had lost her parents so quickly and unexpectedly, it was comforting to belong to a twenty-eight-member family, even if everyone did know her personal information a bit too handily.

Mr. Pennington now looked sadly down at Jacques. "I haven't made a vet appointment yet, but I suppose it's about time," he told Flora. "Most of his problems have to do with simple old age. Like most of my problems," he added, smiling, and Flora smiled with him.

Jacques turned around and made his rheumatic way back across the lawn toward his front door, and Flora continued along Aiken with Daisy, pleased at the day that lay ahead of her: sewing in the morning and an afternoon at Aunt Allie's, taking care of Janie while Allie worked.

One of Flora's favorite things in the entire world was a sewing day — a day, or at least part of a day, in which she could spend time in her room with her patterns and fabrics and sewing machine. Flora's mother had taught her to sew. Flora had, in fact, grown up with sewing. It had been all around her. Her mother had enjoyed it, and then there had been Min and Needle and Thread. When Flora was very little and her family would visit Camden Falls, she had liked nothing better than a trip to her grandmother's sewing store. It had seemed to her as magical a place as a toy shop or a candy counter. Flora would stand in the aisles and finger the laces and the cards of buttons; she would walk between the rows of fabrics and breathe in their scent; and she would gaze at the sewing machines for sale. Later, Needle and Thread was one of the things that had helped Flora to heal after the accident and the loss and the move. Ruby, who couldn't care less about needlework of any kind, and lived instead for singing and performing and the chance to be onstage, had healed in a different way.

On this fine January morning, Flora walked Daisy up and down Aiken Avenue and then ate breakfast with Ruby and Min. Min, whose name was short for Mindy but also for "in a minute," kept checking her watch as they ate. "We're going to have a busy day at the store," she said. "Lots of new merchandise to unpack." She glanced at her granddaughters. "What are your plans today?"

Ruby shrugged. "I don't know about this morning. But I'm going to Lacey's for the afternoon."

Flora cheered silently. Yes! If Ruby was going to Lacey Morris's, then Flora could go to Aunt Allie's and take care of Janie all by herself. She felt absolutely grown-up when she was in charge of the baby.

"Flora? What are your plans?" Min wanted to know.

"Sewing in the morning, Aunt Allie's this afternoon."

The moment breakfast was over, before Min had even left the house, Flora fled to her room, and it was while she was contemplating the crib quilt she was making for Janie that a wonderful idea occurred to her. It started with Janie's quilt, which was to consist of twenty large gingham squares in colors to match her nursery, and which was not taking as long to make as Flora had thought it would. If she had lived in pioneer days, the quilt could have been polished off in one brief bee.

A quilting bee, thought Flora. We could have a

quilting bee at Needle and Thread. If everyone who dropped by made just one or two squares, we would have enough for a large quilt. Then Gigi and Min and I could sew the squares together, and . . .

"Min!" Flora yelped. She ran down the stairs and caught her grandmother as she was putting on her coat. "Min! Don't go yet! I just had a great idea!"

"What on earth?" said Min.

"Did you hear about the community center?" asked Flora breathlessly.

"Flora, honey, I'm going to be late."

"This will just take a second. Did you hear that it might have to close a couple of days a week?"

"I heard that it's having some trouble, yes."

"Well, what if we made a quilt and auctioned it off to raise money for the community center?"

"Made a quilt . . . ?"

"We could have a sort of a quilting bee at Needle and Thread some Saturday. Anyone could drop in to make a square or two and then at the end of the day I'm sure we'd have enough for a quilt. People could make any kind of squares they wanted — simple or complicated — and we'd be there to help. Later, you and Gigi and I would sew them together and make a border and everything, and then we'd auction it off. Don't you think that's a good idea?"

"It'll be a big project but, Flora, yes, I think it's a wonderful idea," said Min, and she gave her grand-daughter a hug. "I'm sorry I have to run, but I promise

I'll talk to Gigi about it today. We'll start making plans."

"Thank you!" Flora exclaimed, and dashed back up the stairs for her morning of sewing.

Flora and Ruby ate their lunch in the kitchen that day. Sometimes on Saturday they liked to walk to College Pizza and buy slices, which they then ate at Needle and Thread with Min. But today they stayed home and ate tuna sandwiches with Daisy Dear staring at them from under the table and King Comma staring at them from the kitchen counter, where technically he shouldn't have been sitting.

"So you're going over to the Morrises' this afternoon?" Flora asked her sister.

"Oh." Ruby swallowed the overly large bite of sandwich she had just stuffed into her mouth. She took a swallow of milk. "No. Lacey forgot she has a dentist appointment. With Dr. Malone. So I'm going to Aunt Allie's with you."

Flora tried hard not to make a face and must have succeeded. "All right," she managed to say.

This was *not* how she had planned to spend her afternoon. She wanted Janie all to herself. But Ruby wasn't allowed to stay at home alone, so Flora had no choice.

When lunch was over and the kitchen had been tidied, and when Daisy Dear had been walked again, Flora and Ruby hopped on their bicycles and rode through Camden Falls to their aunt Allie's house. They hadn't known their aunt well when they were younger, and when she had finally come into their lives a year earlier they had found her stiff and strange, the kind of person who gave you boring gifts such as a contribution to your college account or a certificate saying she'd had a tree named after you in some distant park. But Allie, who was their mother's sister, had softened and had made an effort with her only nieces. Then, lo and behold, she had adopted Janie and brought an infant into their lives — a brand-new baby to hold and dress and play with. She had even named her Jane Marie after Ruby Jane and Flora Marie.

"Can you believe we're riding our bikes in January?" asked Flora as they pedaled along Allie's street.

Ruby shook her head sadly. "Hardly a speck of snow," she said. "Not even one snow day yet. Just flurries. It's pitiful."

"But at least we can ride our bikes. Hey, there are Allie and Janie!"

The girls turned up Allie's driveway, threw down their bicycles, and ran to the house, where their aunt stood at the storm door, cradling Janie.

"Hi!" cried Flora and Ruby, flinging the door open.

There followed a brief argument over who got to hold Janie first, and Flora won. She stroked Janie's soft brown cheek and tickled her palm until her cousin curled her fingers tightly around Flora's thumb.

"We can stay until it starts to get dark," Flora told her aunt, "so you'll have plenty of time to work." She plopped down on the couch and expertly felt Janie's diaper. "Dry," she announced. "Okay, Aunt Allie, you go on to your study. I have everything under control here."

Ruby plopped onto the couch next to Flora. "Yup. Everything's under control."

Allie smiled. "All right. Thank you. This will be wonderful. I'm behind with a few things. My editor will be very happy if I can catch up."

Allie was a writer who had had several books published and who used to live in New York City, the latter fact being a source of fascination for Ruby.

When Allie was settled in her study, the door ajar so that she could hear the baby, just in case, Flora said, "Okay, Ruby, now first you go upstairs and get another outfit for Janie. This one has milk on the front. Choose something cute. And don't forget socks. We don't want her feet to get cold."

"Why does she need clean socks? She doesn't have milk on her socks."

"Because they have to match her outfit!"

"Why don't *you* go get the outfit? I can stay down here and hold Janie."

"Because she looks like she's about to cry, and I know what to do if that happens."

"Well, so do I."

"Ruby? The outfit?"

Ruby stuck her tongue out at Flora and stomped up the stairs. By the time she returned, Janie had fallen asleep in Flora's arms.

"I guess it's nap time already," said Flora, sounding disappointed. She headed for the stairs, Ruby trailing behind her clutching the tiny clothes.

"Well, now what?" asked Ruby a few minutes later when Janie was snoozing in her crib.

"We should make ourselves useful," said Flora. She knocked on the door to Allie's study and poked her head inside. "What would you like us to do?" she asked. "Janie's asleep."

"What? Already? Oh. Well . . . there's a basketful of Janie's laundry that needs to be done. That would be great. Thanks, girls."

Flora tackled the laundry. She finished and Janie was still asleep. "Now what?" she asked Allie.

Allie looked up blearily from her computer. "Um, let's see. I kind of let the recycling go."

Flora directed Ruby in the proper organization of the items to be recycled. Janie slept on. Flora interrupted Allie twice more before she heard the first faint cries from Janie's room. She thundered up the stairs, but Ruby had gotten there first.

"Her head! You have to support her head!" yelped Flora as Ruby lifted the baby from the crib.

"I *am*! I know how to pick her up."

"Well, put her back. She probably needs to be changed."

Reluctantly, Ruby laid her cousin in the crib again. "You sure are bossy," she grumbled.

"I'm not bossy. I just know way more about babies than you do," replied Flora. But she allowed Ruby to change the wet diaper. And to help dress her in the clean outfit. "Doesn't she look *cute*?" Flora cooed when Janie was at last resplendent in a green T-shirt, purple overalls decorated with green alligators, and a pair of green-and-purple-striped socks. She kissed Janie's curly head and carried her down to the living room.

"Let's read to her," suggested Ruby.

So Flora and Ruby read one picture book after another to Janie until the light began to fade and it was time to turn their cousin over to Aunt Allie. As they pedaled back to Aiken Avenue, Flora thought that her day had been nearly perfect.

Boy Trouble

Olivia was worried about something, so she looked up the definition of *boyfriend* in two different dictionaries. One was the dictionary in her computer, which yielded the disturbing explanation: *a man with whom somebody has a romantic relationship.*

It wasn't the word *romantic* that bothered Olivia as much as the word *man.* Why, oh, why, she wondered, was the *boy*friend referred to as a man?

The definition in her parents' unwieldy and well-worn dictionary on the stand in the den was more comforting. 1: *a sweetheart, beau, or escort of a girl or woman* 2: *a boy who is one's friend.*

Well. That was more like it. Olivia much preferred to think of Jacob as merely her escort. (She noted with relief that this definition didn't promote the boy to a man.) "A boy who is one's friend" was even better. Maybe Jacob really was simply a boy who was her friend. But she knew in her heart that when her teenage cousin

Ashley referred to Jacob as Olivia's boyfriend, she did not mean "Jacob, who is Olivia's friend, who happens to be a boy." And certainly when Melody glared at her and Jacob in school it wasn't because she wanted Jacob for her own escort. No, she wanted Jacob for whatever the modern equivalent of *sweetheart* or *beau* might be.

And that was one of the great and unfortunate differences between Olivia and Melody. Olivia, with each passing day, became more convinced that she wanted Jacob for her friend who happened to be a boy, while Melody — and Tanya and probably quite a few other girls at school — wanted him as one of the snappier definitions of *boyfriend*.

The very worst thing of all was that Jacob himself thought that, where Olivia was concerned, he fell more solidly in the sweetheart category than the friend category.

How had this happened? Olivia felt as though she and Jacob were standing on opposite sides of a fence, but she was the only one who knew it.

And now, today, Olivia and Jacob were going out on their very first non-dance date. Just the two of them. Their first official date, in the minds of everyone except Olivia, had been the Halloween dance at school ten weeks earlier. As far as Olivia had been concerned, her friend Jacob (who happened to be a boy) had simply invited her to a dance, which had been thrilling because no other girl in the seventh grade had received an actual invitation. But Olivia had not thought of Jacob as her boyfriend, and she hadn't thought of the dance as a date. Not exactly. The confusing thing was that she had *wondered* if the dance was a date and if Jacob *might* be her boyfriend. But she hadn't been able to tell.

Ten weeks of wondering had gone by, and now Olivia knew two things for sure: 1. Jacob thought of himself as her boyfriend and 2. Olivia was not ready to be anyone's girlfriend.

Then something almost unimaginable had happened. Jacob had phoned one night earlier in the week and had said, "Olivia, would you like to go out on a date?" He had invited her to go to the movies with him on Saturday afternoon.

(That was not the unimaginable thing.)

Olivia had relayed the request to her parents, certain their answer would be no. After all, Olivia had skipped a grade and had a late birthday to boot, so she was nearly two years younger than most of the kids in her class.

"Mom? Dad?" she had said. "Jacob wants to take me to the movies this Saturday. Can I go?"

Perhaps her mistake was that she hadn't actually used the word *date*. In any case, her parents had merely glanced at each other and then her mother had said, "If he's taking you in the afternoon, then yes, you may go."

That was the unimaginable thing.

Olivia had suddenly found herself in Dateland, preparing for the event on Saturday all by herself. She had told Flora and Nikki that she and Jacob were going to a movie over the weekend, but she hadn't told them that Jacob had invited her on a date, so there had been no explosion of excitement. In fact, she was pretty sure they had forgotten about the movie. She had seen Flora and Ruby pedaling down Aiken just after lunch, undoubtedly on their way to see Janie. And when Nikki had phoned Olivia the evening before, it was simply to say that she was surprised she'd been given more than four hours of weekend homework, which seemed like a lot for the first week after vacation.

Olivia leaned on her windowsill and gazed morosely out across her yard. She knew exactly why she hadn't told Flora and Nikki about the date, and now she felt like a liar for keeping the information to herself. She hadn't said anything because she wasn't excited. (Wasn't excited? That was an understatement.) And she knew that if they could see her extreme lack of excitement, then she would have to explain it to them, and she wasn't ready to have that conversation. Not yet.

So Olivia was getting ready for her date/not-a-date by herself. She looked into her wardrobe. She remembered how much thought she had put into the outfit she'd worn to Thanksgiving dinner with her big family. It had taken her days to settle on something. Now she merely glanced at the clothes she was already wearing and decided she needed a clean top. After all, she and Jacob were only going to sit in a darkened theatre. Who would see her? She whisked off her slightly grubby sweatshirt, grabbed the nearest blouse, and slipped it on.

Fine, she thought. She looked just fine.

She realized she felt a teensy bit angry.

It was while she was dragging herself downstairs that she realized what had made her angry. It was the thought of the darkened theatre. The *darkened* theatre. She knew what went on in the darkness during dates. The knowledge made her nervous, and the nervousness made her crabby.

"Bye, Mom!" she called as she reached the front door.

Usually, Olivia's parents worked at Sincerely Yours together, but on Saturdays they sometimes switched off so that one of them could spend time with Olivia and her brothers.

"Have fun, sweetie," her mother replied. "Come home right after the movie."

"Okay," said Olivia, heartily wishing that her parents had forbidden her to go in the first place.

She began the walk to Main Street. At least Jacob hadn't offered to pick her up at home and escort her to the theatre. That would have seemed way too datelike. Olivia had ten more minutes to herself before —

"Olivia! Hi!"

Olivia jerked her head up as she turned onto Dodds Lane.

There was Jacob at the corner of Dodds and Main, leaning casually against the wall of Dutch Haus.

"Hi," Olivia replied, and suddenly she couldn't help smiling, because she *did* like Jacob. He was her good friend who was a boy (which was how all the trouble had started).

Olivia headed to Jacob and they made their way along Main Street, waving at Min and Gigi in Needle and Thread, at Olivia's father and Robby Edwards in Sincerely Yours, where Robby worked part-time, and at the Fongs in their studio. They crossed Main Street, turned right, and continued to the theatre.

Olivia's spirits had risen somewhat, but now they crashed to the ground with a resounding thump: Standing at the ticket window were Melody and Tanya, and as they turned to enter the theatre they caught sight of Olivia and Jacob, and waved. At Jacob. They waved only at Jacob, as if he were standing on the sidewalk all by himself.

Jacob waved back but then touched Olivia's elbow, stepped up to the window, and purchased two tickets. Melody and Tanya, disappointed, trailed into the theatre.

"I have money," said Olivia, pulling several bills out of her pocket.

But Jacob shook his head. "Nope. This is a date and it's my treat." He took both tickets from the cashier, held the door open for Olivia, and handed the tickets to the man at the booth.

"Popcorn?" asked Jacob, and before Olivia could answer, he bought a barrel-size tub of popcorn and a large Coke. He grabbed two straws from the counter and would have taken Olivia by the hand, she thought, except that his were already full.

Olivia wished that Camden Falls was large enough to have a giant multiplex with ten or twelve theatres into which Melody and Tanya might have disappeared. But no, the theatre was big enough for one movie only. Olivia squinted her eyes in the dim light, hoping to spot the girls immediately so that she and Jacob could sit as far from them as possible.

There they were. Smack in the middle of the theatre.

"Let's sit in the front row!" said Olivia brightly.

"The front row?! We'll get carsick if we sit up there," replied Jacob. "That happened to my cousin once and he barfed in the aisle when —"

"Okay, okay," said Olivia. She was whispering, not wanting to attract Melody and Tanya's attention. "Let's sit here."

"In the *back* row?" said Jacob in a rather loud voice.

"Yes! *Shh!*"

But Jacob was already leading her to seats that were just two rows ahead of the vultures, who called out, "Hi, Jacob!"

Jacob and Olivia sat down and wriggled out of their coats, and Jacob placed the Coke in their shared armrest, artfully arranging the straws in the cup.

Olivia looked down at it and was now faced with another problem: the Spit Factor. She glanced unhappily at the two straws sticking out of the one cup. It was really a shame that she thoroughly understood the physics of straws, because the thought of all the soda that was slurped up *as far as* someone's mouth and then fell back into the soda only to be slurped up again later was positively revolting.

Olivia would have to *pretend* to drink the soda.

The popcorn presented a different problem. There was no way Olivia would be able to eat popcorn after Jacob had licked butter and salt from his fingers and then put them slimily back in the bucket. However, it was one thing to pretend to drink Coke; it was another matter to pretend to eat popcorn. She could fake the drinking — thank goodness for her own personal straw. But she didn't know how many times she could put an empty fist to her mouth and chew away on nonexistent popcorn.

Olivia was so caught up in these thoughts that she barely noticed when the lights in the theatre went down. But she certainly noticed when, as soon as the movie started, Jacob's right hand snaked around the cup of soda and crept into her lap. It found Olivia's left hand and, before she knew it, their fingers were laced together.

Olivia wanted desperately to remove her hand from Jacob's, but she didn't want to hurt his feelings. Eventually, she slid her eyes to the left and tried to read the expression on Jacob's face. He was staring straight ahead as if he were . . . well, as if he were watching a movie. How could he act as if holding Olivia's hand was usual? Holding Jacob's hand definitely was not usual for Olivia. It was the opposite of usual. Not only that, it was sweaty.

Olivia was not paying the least bit of attention to the movie. Instead, she focused on whether she could extract her hand from Jacob's without 1. hurting his feelings or 2. giving Melody and Tanya further ammunition in their small but cruel war against her. She was positive they were watching her and Jacob more closely than they were watching the movie, and she didn't want them to think anything was wrong. She *certainly* didn't want them to think she was a baby who had never held a boy's hand, even though that was true.

So Olivia's hand remained sweatily locked in Jacob's until the end of the show. When the lights came on, Jacob sighed, unclasped Olivia's hand, patted it, squished the now empty Coke cup into the now empty popcorn container (Jacob had consumed everything by himself), and held Olivia's coat for her while she slipped it on.

Olivia risked a glance at Melody and Tanya's seats and saw that they were empty, except for all of their trash. Good. They were already gone.

"So," said Jacob a few minutes later as they left the theatre, squinting in the afternoon sunshine, "what did you think?"

Olivia almost said, "About what?" but caught herself in time. "Oh. It was . . . it was *great*. Thank you."

"What was your favorite part?"

What was her favorite part? What kind of question was that?

She was still groping for an answer when Jacob said, "Mine was the scene in the castle."

"Oh. Mine, too."

"Really?"

"Yes?"

"You don't sound very sure."

"Well . . ."

"And that part was pretty bloody."

"Right."

"Olivia, is something wrong?"

"No! What could be wrong?"

"I don't know. You just seem kind of distant."

Olivia shrugged.

"Do you want to go to College Pizza?"

"I can't. I promised Mom I'd come home right after the movie."

"Oh. Okay."

Olivia heard the hurt in his voice, but she didn't know what to do about it. A block and a half later, as they stood awkwardly in front of Fig Tree, she said, "Thanks, Jacob. I had fun. It was nice of you to treat me."

Jacob smiled.

"See you on Monday," called Olivia as she turned to cross Main Street.

"See you."

Olivia walked home quickly and went directly to her room, pausing just long enough to say, "Yeah," when her mother asked if she had had fun. Then she sat at her desk and considered phoning Flora to discuss the horrifying date and all that had gone wrong, but she didn't know how to explain her feelings. And anyway, she'd been able to tell, just by walking by Flora's house, that no one was home yet. It had given off an air of emptiness.

CHAPTER 4

The Self-improvement Plan

There were a number of rules in the Northrop household, and one of them was that homework was to be done at the kitchen table or at one's desk. Min was a firm believer that sitting up at a table or desk helped with focus. And posture. Flora, who had almost never broken a rule on purpose, was downstairs dutifully doing her homework at the kitchen table on Wednesday afternoon. Ruby was upstairs working in a reclining position on her bed. She didn't care. Min wasn't home to see her. And Ruby didn't really understand the benefit of sitting at a desk. Her mind could wander just as easily at her desk as it could anywhere else. And her posture was already perfect.

Ruby patted her stuffed animals and straightened the necktie on Bun, her pink rabbit. She leaned over and felt under the bed to see if the gum she had stuck there was as hard as a rock yet. Not quite. She could still press her fingernail into it. Maybe in another two weeks it would be petrified.

She resettled herself on the bed, lay against the pillows, and turned the pages in the geology chapter of her fifth-grade science book. She was supposed to be reading about sedimentation and erosion and layers of dirt, but the chapter on mammals was much more interesting, so she studied the photos in it.

Mammals made her think of animals, and animals made her glance at her dresser, on which sat her collection of china animals. It really was quite a collection, thought Ruby. She let the book slide out of her hands and tried to count the animals from her spot on the bed. She had added to them considerably since she and Flora had moved to Camden Falls. This was mostly because across the street from Needle and Thread was a store called Stuff 'n' Nonsense, which, although it was owned by an absolutely horrible old woman named Mrs. Grindle, had a very good selection of china animals, and Ruby had spent quite a bit of her allowance money in there. She now had a china ibex and a china camel and a china elephant and a china fox and a china rhino and fifty-six other animals, including her newest purchase, a china polar bear.

Ruby sighed. Her homework was not going well. She got to her feet, stood in her room for a few moments, and just listened. When she and her sister had first moved to Camden Falls, it had taken Ruby a while to become accustomed to the sounds of the Row Houses. There was steam heat, for one thing, and squirrels running along the roof, and the noises from the houses on either side of theirs. Ruby's bedroom shared a wall with Olivia's bedroom next door, and occasionally Ruby could hear voices or laughter or faint music. All very different from the sounds of the house in which she had grown up.

But at the moment, Ruby didn't notice these things. She listened instead for sounds from the first floor. She heard nothing. Good. Perfect Flora was undoubtedly still at work in the kitchen, sitting up straight in her chair.

Ruby tiptoed to her doorway and listened again. She stepped into the hallway and listened. She walked five steps toward the back of the house and listened. When she still heard nothing, she slipped into Min's bedroom.

"Drawers," Ruby said to herself, and nodded.

There was a total of eight drawers in Min's room: four in her bureau, three in her desk, and one in her nightstand. Now would be a good time to explore them. Grown-ups' drawers were usually interesting. Sometimes they were boring, like the top drawer in her father's bureau, which she had long ago waited patiently to explore and then had found to hold only neatly folded pairs of socks and a rock that Flora had painted when she was three. But mostly they were interesting. She had discovered that in the very back of her mother's middle desk drawer had been a box containing all of her mom's old report cards and also a fascinating plastic pin in the shape of a beetle, with black cords for legs and bobbling wire antennae. Ruby had secretly worn the pin at dinner one night, hidden under her sweater, before replacing it in the drawer. And she had read the report cards, lingering over such phrases as "a delight to teach" and "needs to work on class participation — we would like to hear Frannie's voice!"

Where were her mother's report cards now? wondered Ruby. She wanted to read them again, especially since she attended the very same school at which her mother had once been a student. And where was the bug pin?

Ruby glanced over her shoulder before gently sliding Min's top bureau drawer open. She gasped.

Underwear! And not regular old-lady underwear, but rather large old-lady underwear. Well, Min *was* on the large side. But Ruby hadn't expected her underpants to be quite so . . .

She held up a pair and then slipped both of her legs into one opening. I'll bet Lacey and I could wear this pair together! thought Ruby.

Ruby replaced the panties and then rummaged carefully through the rest of the drawers in the bureau, but apart from containing a lot of plus-size articles of clothing, the contents weren't particularly interesting.

The small drawer in the nightstand revealed only

the remote control for the ceiling fan, a bag of almonds, and two bookmarks. But the bottom drawer of the desk was a different story. Behind all the neatly stacked folders labeled NEEDLE AND THREAD (Ruby had a vague idea that they might contain tax returns) was a cardboard shoe box, the lid held in place with a fat rubber band.

Aha! thought Ruby, and she sat back on her haunches and pulled out the box. She tackled the rubber band gingerly, afraid it might snap apart and hit her in the face. But the band was new and nicely pliant. Ruby set it on the floor and lifted the lid. Inside were a collection of objects that looked familiar — a silver letter opener; a round wooden box with a sheep painted on the top and a penny from 1966 (the year of her mother's birth) inside; a small crystal owl, its wings extended in flight; a half-empty bottle of perfume; and a perfectly shaped snail shell. But it wasn't until Ruby saw the plastic bug with the string legs and the wire antennae that she recognized the items as having belonged to her mother. In a flash, she could picture each one in its spot in her old house. The letter opener on her mother's desk, the perfume bottle on her bureau, the owl next to the perfume . . .

Ruby ran her finger over the smooth, cool surface of the owl and then lifted it gently from the box. She held it in her hand and saw tiny rainbows on the surface as she turned it in the light.

This was my mother's, thought Ruby, and Min is

hiding it in her desk. (Ruby conveniently forgot that her mother was Min's daughter.) Min has all these keepsakes that were Mom's and I have . . . She considered. Well, she actually did have a number of things. Min had made certain that Ruby and Flora had been given several items that had belonged to their parents. Ruby had a photo album that her mother had kept when she was Ruby's age and a bracelet her mother had loved and worn nearly every day, but she didn't have anything nearly as spectacular as the crystal owl.

Ruby set the owl on the floor and cocked her head to listen. She heard a creak and jumped, her knee connecting with the box and causing an alarming rattling sound. She leaped to her feet, fully expecting to find Flora standing accusingly in Min's doorway, but everything was silent again. Ruby hurriedly replaced the rubber band on the box, stashed the box in the back of the drawer again, and closed the drawer. The owl still lay on the floor.

Ruby picked it up. She would just borrow it, she thought, like she had borrowed the bug and worn it to dinner. She carried the owl down the hall to her room and stood in front of her bureau. "Animals," she said, "I want you to meet a new friend." She held the owl aloft. "This is Owlie. He's been stuffed away in a box for about a year and a half, poor thing. It's really tragic. Polar Bear, you're the newcomer here. I want you to make Owlie feel welcome." It was while Ruby was rearranging the animals that her hand slipped and she dropped the owl. She watched as, in horrible slow motion, it hit the edge of her metal wastebasket and then landed squarely on the eight-inch strip of wooden floor between the edge of her rug and the wall.

The little owl now lay in three jagged pieces, the wings broken off of the body amid a handful of smaller shards.

"Uh-oh," said Ruby. And when she heard Flora climbing the stairs, she added, "Yipes."

"Ruby?" called her sister.

Ruby slammed her door shut. "Just a minute!"

"What are you doing?"

"Nothing."

"I need to ask you something."

Ruby opened the door two inches. "What?"

Flora frowned and tried to peer into the room. "What do you want for dinner? Min said to start something before she gets home."

"Spaghetti," Ruby replied, and closed the door firmly.

She sat on her bed and stared at the mess. "Okay," she said to herself as Flora's footsteps retreated. "Okay. This is going to be all right. First things first. Clean up the mess."

Ruby retrieved the dustpan and broom that Min kept in her sewing room and swept the pieces of crystal into a bag, which she would dispose of very carefully later on so that no one would get cut.

Now, how to replace the owl? For that was what Ruby had already decided she must do: replace the owl before Min realized it was gone. Ruby was certain Min looked in the box from time to time (that was why the rubber band was new), so simply pretending the event hadn't taken place was out of the question. The owl would be missed eventually. But Ruby thought she had some time in which to make the switch, perhaps even several months. The question was whether the owl could actually *be* replaced. Certainly Stuff 'n' Nonsense didn't carry anything like it, but maybe one of the fancier stores on Main Street did. Ruby would check all of the gift stores as well as the new jewelry store. If necessary, she could also check the stores out at the mall someday.

Ruby's heart, which had been beating very fast, began to slow down. But she continued to sit on her bed and think. She had been in a bit of trouble recently. Actually, more than just a bit. She had nearly gotten herself expelled from the Children's Chorus back in November for not attending rehearsals and subsequently making a mess of one of her solos in the Thanksgiving concert. In the end, although she hadn't been expelled, she had very embarrassingly been put on probation. Furthermore, her grades, which had always been mediocre at best, had been slipping even further, and just the previous week, when school had started again, her teacher had called Min and arranged for a special conference, reminding her that Ruby would soon be in sixth grade, with a heavier workload and more responsibilities. Was Ruby prepared for that? Min had returned home and had quite a talk with Ruby that evening.

Miserably, Ruby began to list her other faults: She didn't listen to adults, she was careless, she was messy, she was impulsive, she didn't plan ahead, and evidently she had a tendency to be rude.

"Well, I'm going to take care of all that," Ruby now said aloud.

She jumped up and made her way to her desk. The fact that she couldn't find anything in the stew of junk there made her more determined than ever to take matters in hand.

"I will draw up a self-improvement plan," she announced. "And I'll start off the list with: Be neater."

To that end, Ruby threw away all the gum wrappers and stray scraps of paper littering the surface of her desk. She stowed her pencils and pens and markers in the top drawer, and put all the nondesk items (jewelry, candy, clothing) in their proper places in her room. At last she sat down, pulled a pen and a sheet of paper from the recently tidied drawer, and wrote: *Ruby Northrop's Personal and Private Self-improvement Plan. THIS IS SERIOUS.*

Ruby began her list. It took her ten minutes to complete it and she was quite pleased with it.

1. *Be neater.*
2. *Go to all lessons and rehearsals unless I am sick.*
3. *Plan ahead. (Ask someone how to do that.)*
4. *Finish homework on time.*
5. *Practice lessons (chorus, tap) at home.*
6. *Listen to adults and then actually do what they say.*
7. *Try very hard not to be rude. If I slip up, I should apologize right away.*
8. *Check my work before I hand it in.*
9. *Think before I act.*

(Previously, Ruby had been under the impression that this last bit of advice referred to acting on the stage, but now she realized it had a different meaning, and that maybe it would even help her to plan ahead.)

10. *Become the Doer of Unpleasant Jobs again.*

In November, when Ruby had realized she needed to earn some money to buy Christmas presents, she had started a small business. She had become the Doer of Unpleasant Jobs and had distributed flyers to her neighbors announcing that she was available to do all those unappealing chores people tended to put off: cleaning out basements and storage rooms, washing windows, organizing shelves, and so forth. Her business had gotten off to a good start, but Ruby had let it lapse after she had earned enough money to buy gifts for Min and Flora and Aunt Allie and Janie and several of her friends and neighbors.

Now, Ruby realized, she would have to get her business up and running again. She had a feeling that a crystal owl (should she be able to find one identical to the one she'd broken) would not be cheap. Certainly it would cost more than $6.71, which was the sum total of Ruby's cash that afternoon.

Ruby had her work cut out for her.

But as she sat on the bed amid her unfinished homework (which she now realized she would have to complete, and complete properly, before she went to sleep that night) she felt calm. Calm and rather grown-up. The accident with the owl had been bad, but it had awakened something in Ruby that had led her to address her problems in a very adult manner. The only sad thing was that she couldn't tell anyone about the self-improvement plan, or at least not the reason behind it. That would have to remain a secret.

Oh, well, thought Ruby. I guess that's part of growing up, too. Sometimes you do something just because you have to, even if you're the only person who knows how great it is.

And she lugged her books to her desk and sat down to begin her assignments.

CHAPTER 5

A Peek in the Windows

If you were to view Camden Falls, Massachusetts, from above, you might think it was a sleepy town. And if you breezed by the exit for Camden Falls on the highway and noticed the sign reading POPULATION: 14,767 (the sign isn't accurate, but for heaven's sake, it can't be updated every time someone is born or dies or moves to or from town), you would think it was a small town. And it is small. And maybe it's sleepy compared to cities. But that doesn't mean it's lacking in drama. A thousand small dramas are unfolding in the town at any moment on any day.

Come and take a look at Camden Falls on this afternoon in early January in what, so far, has been an unusually warm winter. Start your tour on the outskirts of town, where Nikki Sherman and her family live. Today is Friday, and Nikki has been simultaneously looking forward to this day and dreading it. She's been looking forward to the return of her beloved brother, Tobias. He's been back at school for a scant two weeks since the holidays, but Nikki always misses him when he's away, and now he'll be home again in less than an hour. On the other hand, she's been dreading today because it's the last one before her father will return and (Nikki is quite certain) send her family into turmoil. Nikki stands at the front window of her careworn house and stares across the barren yard to the county road, which she can barely make out in the distance. If she were to look to the right and left, or to stare out a back window of the house, she would see more of the same barrenness: a leafless tree here and there, the colorless hollow stalks of grasses that in the summer are green and supple, a hedgerow, a shack. It's lonely sometimes out here in the country — but Nikki wouldn't want to live anywhere else. She reaches down to pat Paw-Paw's head and then squints her eyes. Has a car turned off the county road and onto her lane? She stares. Yes! Tobias is back early. Nikki and Paw-Paw fly out the door and are waiting to greet him before he has even pulled to a stop.

The weather is mild, as every single person in Camden Falls has been noting for weeks now, so you won't mind a walk through the country in the direction of Camden Falls. Step carefully, keep your eyes open, and you'll probably see deer, maybe a skunk or a possum, definitely squirrels and birds of many kinds, and if you're lucky you'll spot a fox or a coyote. Nikki saw a mink one memorable winter day.

Pass the turnoff for Minnewaska State Park, pass Al's Produce Stand (closed for the winter), pass The Blue Barn (antiques), and now you'll see more and more roads intersecting with the county road. A few more blocks and you'll reach Main Street. But stop a couple of blocks before Main Street, turn left, then right, and you'll find yourself standing before what can only be described as a cottage. The small house surrounded by gardens looks as though it should be the home of an elf or a fairy. The youngest children in town actually believe that, and then they grow up and learn that the old woman who lives there all alone is practically a recluse, and some of them call her Scary Mary. Scary Mary, who isn't scary at all, works several days a week at Needle and Thread, and has recently learned that after decades of thinking she was an only child with no relatives other than her mother (her father left her and her mother when Mary was a baby), she in fact has a large extended family, including a younger half sister, who contacted her on Thanksgiving Day. Mary is going to meet part of her family soon. Eight of them will be coming to visit her. Mary never dreamed that at the age of nearly eighty her life would change in this impossibly wonderful way. Maybe she really is a character in a fairy story.

You're just a few blocks from Main Street now, so you might as well stroll along it. It is, after all, the heart of town. Camden Falls might be small and even a little old-fashioned, but it is not unchanging. While some of the stores and businesses have been around for decades — the movie theatre, Needle and Thread, Fig Tree, Zinder's — others are new. Sincerely Yours opened less than a year ago, the diner opened in the fall, and just before the holidays a magic shop opened. As the economy declines (a topic the adults discuss endlessly and the children try to ignore), other businesses are struggling. The shoe store is about to close, and other stores will surely follow. Still, Main Street is a pleasant place, and on a winter afternoon, a cozy one as well. Old friends are meeting at Frank's Beans for a cup of coffee or greeting one another in front of the post office. Store windows shine, and the lampposts are wound with tiny gold lights. Walk as far north as Dutch Haus, turn left onto Dodds Lane, then right onto Aiken Avenue, and there before you are the Row Houses, where Nikki occasionally imagines herself living along with Flora and Ruby and Olivia.

The Row Houses take up a good portion of the street just off of Dodds. While they were once populated by Camden Falls's wealthiest families, families who could afford maids for the maids' rooms (not to mention gardeners and chauffeurs), the people who live in them now have turned the maids' rooms into offices and playrooms, and they do their own gardening and driving.

The small dramas of Camden Falls are unfolding here on Aiken Avenue, too. In the second house from the left live the Hamiltons — Willow Hamilton, who's a friend of Flora and Olivia, her little brother, Cole, and their parents. Mrs. Hamilton, however, has been absent from the house since the unforgettable evening before Thanksgiving when the police were called to the Hamilton residence and Mrs. Hamilton, after years of unstable behavior, was taken to a hospital for treatment. Willow and Cole were sad at first, and then relieved. Their home has been a steadier and happier place since she left. Willow misses having a mother, but she doesn't miss her mother's unpredictable and mysterious house rules, and now, less than two months since that night, she feels a peace that she wonders if most people feel every day without recognizing its extraordinariness. She looks out her window and sees Cole playing in the yard with Bessie, their dog, and the Morris boys from next door. Cole is tearing after Mathias and Travis in a game that looks like tag but that Willow thinks the boys have made up this afternoon.

To the right of the Hamiltons' house is the one belonging to the Malones — Dr. Malone, a dentist, and his daughters, Margaret and Lydia, who are in high school. Margaret spent the autumn busily applying to colleges, and she has just learned that she's been accepted at her first choice: Smith College in North-ampton, Massachusetts. Margaret won't be traveling far to go to her new school, and yet Northampton feels worlds away. To begin with, it's twice the size of Camden Falls. But what Margaret is thinking as she lies on her bed, trying to process the news she's just received, is that she will soon be a *college* student — at what she believes is the perfect college. For her, anyway. A college with an art museum and a theatre department and more courses than she can imagine. She plans to take classes in writing and psychology and history and the history of art. She loves Camden Falls, but she can't wait to start her new life in Northampton.

Next door to Margaret, Flora, alone in her house, is sitting at the sewing machine in her bedroom. She's decided to start her weekend homework on Saturday. For now she wants to do nothing but sew, and she's finishing the inseam on a pair of corduroy rompers for Janie. Seated at the machine in the quiet of her house on a late winter afternoon, Flora feels a calm settle over her.

Walking slowly to the door of the third house from the right are Rudy Pennington and Jacques. Mr. Pennington's pace is due not to his stiff joints but to the news he got when he took Jacques to the vet this morning. The doctor, a woman Mr. Pennington likes and trusts — she's been Jacques's vet since he was a puppy — has told him that Jacques probably doesn't have many weeks left to live. And Mr. Pennington is wondering how on earth he will be able to say goodbye to his companion.

"Come on, boy," says Mr. Pennington, and he holds the door open so Jacques can limp inside.

CHAPTER 6

Escape

Nikki lay in bed, holding her breath and listening. She wondered how much time she had spent listening in her house: listening for the sound of her father's footsteps on the stairs late at night, for the sound of angry hushed voices from her parents' room, and especially for the sound of tires crunching gravel on the lane to her house. Tires on gravel were the worst sound of all, because they signaled an end to a peaceful time, even if it had been only an hour or so, when her father had been blessedly absent from the house. For a year now, Nikki had been able to replace her worried listening with other more productive activities. But this morning was different. This morning her father would be returning. And so Nikki was once again listening for tires on gravel.

"Nikki? How many more minutes until he gets here?" Mae said sleepily from the bed across the room.

"I don't know," replied Nikki. "It's still early. He won't be here for a while, anyway." But Nikki wasn't sure about that, which was why she was listening.

There was no response from Mae, so Nikki tossed back her covers and padded barefoot across the chilly floor to her sister's bed. "Mae?"

"I heard you."

"Well, come on, get up. Let's go downstairs and have breakfast with Mom and Tobias."

"I don't want him to hurt Mom," said Mae. And Nikki understood that Mae was talking about their father.

"Tobias won't let anything happen," replied Nikki, trying to sound confident.

Nikki spent a considerable amount of time that morning listening. Everyone in her family was on edge. Mae sat on the floor and stared distractedly at the television, and when Paw-Paw walked in front of her, she swatted his rump and said, "Get out of my way!"

"Mae!" exclaimed Mrs. Sherman. "That is not how we treat living creatures."

"It's how your husband treats us," muttered Mae.

"Not while I'm here," said Tobias, darkening.

"Enough," said Mrs. Sherman. "Stop it, all of you." (Nikki had said nothing, but this wasn't the time to point that out.)

Mae, glowering, got to her feet and kicked an armchair.

"Do you need a time-out?" Mrs. Sherman asked her.

"No." But Mae disappeared up the stairs anyway.

And that was when Nikki finally did hear gravel crunching. "He's here," she whispered.

"Better put Paw-Paw outside," said Mrs. Sherman, and Nikki whisked him out the side door. "Stay, boy," she commanded softly.

Mae had run back down the stairs and was peering out a window. After a few moments, she left the window to turn and press her face into her mother's waist, as if she were a toddler.

Nikki, who was now listening for the sound of a knock on the door, was so startled when the door suddenly opened that she actually let out a cry.

"I'm home, everybody!" announced Mr. Sherman. He set down two shopping bags, closed the door behind him, and shrugged out of his coat. And then he stood by the door, his arms dangling at his sides.

No one moved. No one spoke. The Shermans formed an uncomfortable picture. In those few seconds before the strange spell was broken, Nikki studied her father and was surprised by what she saw. He was dressed neatly and he was wearing a jacket. No necktie, but a jacket and a clean white shirt and corduroy pants. *Corduroy* pants. Where were his falling-apart jeans? Where was his stained T-shirt? And where had the jacket come from? She noted that his hair was clean and that he had combed it, leaving noticeable comb tracks on either side of the part. His nails had been trimmed and he had shaved that morning. Also, he was growing a mustache.

"Well," said Mr. Sherman at last. "This is some greeting."

Nikki glanced at Tobias and saw him tense.

"Cat got your tongue?" Mr. Sherman asked Mae, who nodded.

Otherwise, no one moved.

"Hi, Dad," said Nikki finally.

"I got something for you," Mr. Sherman told her. "Got presents for all of you."

Mae released herself from her mother's waist. "Presents?"

At this, Nikki and Tobias smiled, and Mrs. Sherman said nervously, "Well, that got her attention."

Mr. Sherman began to remove items from one of the shopping bags.

"Are *both* bags full of presents?" asked Mae incredulously. She leaned in for a closer look.

"Why don't we sit down?" said Mrs. Sherman.

They sat around the kitchen table, and Nikki's father handed out gifts as if he were Santa Claus. The presents weren't wrapped, but Nikki didn't care. She found herself feeling as incredulous as Mae looked. Their father had never bought gifts for any occasion.

He hadn't remembered birthdays; he hadn't even bought Christmas gifts.

"Here you go, Tobias," said Mr. Sherman, pulling a heavy green sweatshirt from the first bag.

"Wow," said Tobias softly.

"And this is for you, Nikki." He handed her a small box. When Nikki opened it, she found a pair of silver earrings inside. They weren't for pierced ears, but they were pretty, and Nikki thought she might be able to wear them anyway. "Thank you," she said politely.

Mr. Sherman reached for the bottom of the bag and finally withdrew a box of perfume, which he handed Nikki's mother.

Mae was now eyeing the second bag. Her father set it on the floor next to her chair. "Everything in there's for you."

Mae's eyes widened. "Everything?" She scrambled from her chair, knelt on the floor, and began pulling things from the bag — a princess costume, a book about horses, a sticker book, and finally an elaborate doll. "This is for me, too?" she asked, cradling it and gazing fondly into its face. "Really? This is for me?"

"Who else would a doll be —" Mr. Sherman started to say, but then he caught himself. "For my special girl," he said instead, and patted Mae's shoulder.

It was on the tip of Nikki's tongue to ask why her father had given so much to Mae, but she remained silent. Maybe it was okay. Mae was little, and she was fun to shop for. Still, an annoying mosquito of a thought was buzzing around in Nikki's head, demanding to be caught. And examined.

"Well," said Mr. Sherman, "I guess I better get a move on. It's going to take a while to go through everything. I'll start in the bedroom. I've got empty suitcases in the truck. Do you have any boxes?"

"A few," replied Mrs. Sherman, and Nikki's parents disappeared upstairs.

Mae sat on the floor in the living room, the doll at her side. She looked through her new book. She made a picture using the stickers. Then she undressed the doll and dressed it again. "These are the fanciest clothes I've ever seen," she remarked.

The doll was fairly fancy, too, with silky brown hair, a painted face, eyes that opened and closed, and real eyelashes.

"Look, Nikki. The dress has lace on it. Oh, and there are tiny pearl buttons on her shoes!" Mae was glowing. At last she exclaimed, "Daddy's nice!"

Nikki glanced at Tobias. She could feel something tighten in her chest. But Tobias said nothing, so Nikki merely peered out the side door to check on Paw-Paw, who was lying patiently in the winter-brown grass, and who looked dolefully at her but didn't move.

Mr. Sherman ate lunch with his family, a hurried affair of tomato soup and peanut butter sandwiches. Then he slipped his coat on. "Going into town to meet with my lawyer," he said, "but I'll be back in a couple of hours."

"I'll find some boxes for you while you're gone," said Tobias.

"That would be helpful," replied Mr. Sherman, but Nikki noted that he wasn't smiling and she realized something about his eyes. They could bore into you with the hard, calculating stare of a snake. Nikki shivered and looked away, but Tobias held his father's gaze.

"Bye, Daddy!" called Mae as Mr. Sherman hustled out the door.

The second his pickup truck had disappeared from view, Nikki let Paw-Paw back into the house. "Poor old boy," she said, and gave him two biscuits.

"Mommy, Daddy gave me the best presents!" exclaimed Mae.

"You're very lucky," her mother replied.

Two hours later, Mr. Sherman returned, and Tobias met him at the door with a stack of cartons he'd found in a shed.

"How did the meeting go?" asked Mrs. Sherman.

"Why don't you come upstairs with me and I'll fill you in?"

Nikki wandered around her yard. She wanted to put food out for the stray dogs but knew she would have to wait until the evening, until after her father had left. He was staying . . . Where was he staying?

Nikki wasn't sure. With friends? She didn't remember her father having any friends, except for the men he sometimes drank with. Well, maybe he was staying with one of them. She wondered how long it would take him to sort through all of his things. There were closets and shelves and the storage room. He kept tools in one of the sheds. It could take a while. Days. And then there were to be more meetings with the lawyers. She looked at her watch. Her father had been back for just several hours and already it felt like weeks.

The afternoon was growing dark. When Nikki saw a light go on in the living room, she went back inside. Her mother was sitting on the couch, Mae at her feet with the doll.

"Mom? Can I talk to you?" asked Nikki.

"Sure."

"I mean, in private."

They went upstairs to Nikki and Mae's room. Mrs. Sherman sat on Mae's bed and Nikki closed the door. She felt tears threatening to fall and wanted to feel her mother's arms around her. Instead, she stood in front of the bed, feet planted, and said firmly, "Mom, I want to know what's going on with the custody arrangements."

Mrs. Sherman glanced at the door. "Nikki," she said in a whisper, "I think it would be better if we talked about this later. When your father has left."

"But Mom —" Nikki could feel a pounding that started in her head and moved down to her chest.

"What happened when he talked with his lawyer today?"

"Seriously. We'll discuss it later."

"Denise!" roared Mr. Sherman from down the hall, and Nikki's mother winced.

"Later. I promise." She kissed Nikki on the head and hurried from the room.

Nikki flopped onto her bed, sighing immensely, and reached for *A Tree Grows in Brooklyn*, which she was reading for the next meeting of the seventh-grade book club. Nikki was entranced by the story of Francie Nolan and her family, of their lives in Brooklyn at the beginning of the twentieth century. But she found herself unable to escape into their world when it seemed possible that her own world was about to collapse.

"Now?" said Nikki the moment she could hear her father's truck roar to life. It was past the Shermans' usual dinnertime, Mae was hungry and overtired, and everyone was crabby after the long, strained day.

"As soon as dinner's over," Mrs. Sherman said wearily. "Mae needs to eat. We all do."

Nikki waited until the food had been eaten, the table cleared, the dishes washed. Then she glanced at her mother with raised eyebrows.

"All right," said Mrs. Sherman. "Let's go back to your room."

Mae was engrossed in her doll again, seated on the

couch in the living room, caressing the silky hair. "I think I'll name you Peppy," she said softly. She didn't glance up as Nikki and Mrs. Sherman left the kitchen.

"Mom, please tell me that Dad isn't going to get custody of us," Nikki said desperately, the moment her door was closed. This time she sat next to her mother on Mae's bed.

"I can't make any promises," her mother replied. "I don't want to do that until every last piece of paper has been signed. But I am fairly certain that I am going to have full custody of you and Mae."

"Me and Mae?!" cried Nikki in alarm. "What about Tobias?"

"Oh, honey. I didn't mean to scare you." Mrs. Sherman pulled Nikki closer to her. "Tobias is an adult. The custody arrangements apply only to you and Mae."

Nikki relaxed against her mother. "I thought . . . I thought we were going to be separated."

"No. Tobias will stay in college and come home to us on vacations."

"And Mae and I won't ever have to see Dad again?"

"Like I said, I don't want to make any promises yet. But if I do wind up with full custody — and I expect to —" added Mrs. Sherman hastily, seeing the look on Nikki's face, "then you and Mae won't have to visit your father unless you want to. It will be up to you."

Nikki tried to feel relieved. But she was afraid that if she let relief trickle in, then something would go very, very wrong. The mosquito was buzzing inside her head again, and she really needed to examine it. Long after her mother had left the room, Nikki lay on her bed and tried to capture the mosquito, tried to identify what, specifically, had troubled her that day. Not the thought of custody arrangements going awry. Not her father's unsettling presence in the house. Mae? The gifts?

No. It was two words:

Daddy's nice.

CHAPTER 7

Good-bye, Old Friend

Rudy Pennington had begun nearly every day of
Jacques's long life by sitting next to him on the couch
in the living room and holding a Morning Discussion.
Jacques, who was allowed anywhere in the Row House
and on any surface, would position himself on the
middle cushion and look seriously into Rudy's face
while Rudy stroked his ears and told him about the day
to come.

"You're going to like today, boy," Mr. Pennington
might say. "Lots of company, and I think we'll walk
into town after lunch. Maybe we'll visit Min at Needle
and Thread. And, let me see, after that we'll stop in the
Cheshire Cat before we go home. We'll pick up some
more biscuits for you."

On Sunday, the day after Nikki's father had
arrived, Jacques joined Mr. Pennington on the couch
as usual, but he didn't sit at attention. He lay in the

crack between two cushions, his head drooping over the edge.

"Jacques?" said Rudy. "Not feeling very well today?"

Jacques rolled his eyes toward Rudy.

"Do you want a belly rub?"

Jacques glanced away.

Mr. Pennington rested his hand on Jacques's head. "All right. We'll have a quiet day, then. Let's see if you want any breakfast."

In the kitchen, Mr. Pennington spooned Turkey 'n' Sweet Potato Feast from a can and stirred in some kibble. He set the bowl on the floor and then refilled Jacques's water dish.

"Jacques!" he called. "Breakfast!" He remembered the days when Jacques would hop up and down at his feet, snuffling and woofing, while Rudy prepared the food. How long since he had done that? How long since he had eaten his meals with such speed that Mr. Pennington would say to him, "My word, did you inhale that?"

"Jacques?" called Mr. Pennington again. He picked up the dish, intending to carry it into the living room and allow Jacques to eat on the couch, but suddenly there was the old dog making his way into the kitchen. Mr. Pennington set the bowl on the floor again and stood above Jacques, watching. "Do you think you can eat?" he asked.

Jacques looked up at Rudy as if to say, "I'll try," and then sniffed cautiously at his dish. At last he sat on his haunches, his left leg sliding to the side, and took a delicate mouthful.

"Good boy," whispered Mr. Pennington.

Jacques tried another mouthful.

Ten minutes later, the dish still half full, Jacques sat back from his laborious chewing.

"Is that it?" asked Ruby. "You don't want any more? You did pretty well, old boy. We'll save the rest. Maybe you'll want it later."

Ten days, the vet had said. Jacques had two weeks, maybe three, left. He was old, and he was giving out, pure and simple.

Jacques hobbled back to the living room, gathered himself to jump onto the couch again, slipped, and fell on his rump. He turned wounded eyes to Mr. Pennington. In an instant, Rudy had gathered him in his arms and lifted him onto the cushion.

"You sit here," Rudy told Jacques. "I'm going to make some coffee and read with you for a while."

Mr. Pennington had read several chapters in *The Peterkin Papers*, by Lucretia P. Hale (which Min had told him was her favorite book when she was a little girl, and if it had been Min's favorite, then Rudy wanted to experience it), when Jacques suddenly awakened, looking perkier, and jumped to the floor on his own.

"Feeling better?" asked Mr. Pennington.

Jacques headed for the kitchen, moving at a

noticeably faster clip. Mr. Pennington followed him. When Jacques stopped at the back door, tail wagging in a tentative manner, and looked up at the man who had been his friend for so long, Rudy opened the door and Jacques ambled outside.

"What a nice day," remarked Mr. Pennington. "Hardly feels like January. This could be a morning in October. Or March." He tipped his head back to feel the sun on his skin, thinking that dogs like to be sun-warmed as much as people do.

When Jacques had made his way down the steps and into the yard, Mr. Pennington said, "Let me get my jacket and we'll take a little walk."

For the next half an hour, Rudy and Jacques toured the backyard of the Row House. Jacques stopped in all his favorite places, and Rudy joined him. They sat on the bench and Rudy said, "Remember when there were three of us sitting here? Old man, old woman, and you? You were a pup then. Those were nice days."

Jacques stopped under an oak tree and Mr. Pennington peered up into its stark branches. "You almost caught a squirrel one day," he said, "but it escaped up this tree. You were moving so fast, I thought you'd run right up the trunk after it."

Jacques sniffed at the remains of Mr. Pennington's vegetable garden. "You used to like to garden with me," remarked Rudy. "You'd sit out here while I planted and weeded. And you liked to eat green beans. Remember that? And to play with the vines?"

Jacques settled himself between two rosebushes. "Another of your favorite spots," said Mr. Pennington, "although how you sat here so often without getting pricked by the thorns is beyond me."

Jacques struggled to his feet and headed for the back door.

"Time to go in?" asked Rudy. "Let's get you a biscuit."

Inside, Mr. Pennington took a cookie from the jar of doggie treats, and Jacques ate it, tail wagging.

"Ha," said Mr. Pennington with a smile. "You're going to prove that doctor wrong. What does she know about your spirit?"

Jacques gave Rudy a grin and headed for the living room. Mr. Pennington remained in the kitchen, cleaning up his breakfast dishes and thinking about what to fix for supper.

He heard a sharp intake of air from beyond the kitchen door.

"Jacques?" Rudy paused to listen. "Jacques?"

He stepped into the dining room and saw Jacques lying on the floor.

As Jacques had grown older, Rudy had wondered if one day the old dog might die in his sleep, and whether Rudy would be able to distinguish sleep from death. Now he saw that death looked very different from sleep. Jacques was lying absolutely still, legs stretched before him, tongue protruding slightly, eyes open.

There was nothing sleeplike about the rigid, surprised posture.

"Well, boy." Mr. Pennington's voice caught and he raised a trembling hand to his lips. Then he bent over and stroked Jacques's body, feeling not lifelessness, but something between life and death. No beating heart, but warmth, and that silky fur, and Jacques's particular musky scent.

At last Mr. Pennington straightened up and reached for the telephone. "Min," he said. "Jacques is gone." He listened for a moment. "Thank you."

Min arrived at Mr. Pennington's house two minutes later. She put her arms around her friend and held him close.

"I called the vet," said Rudy, dabbing at his eyes with a limp handkerchief. "The office isn't open today, but she'll meet us there anyway."

"We'll take my car," said Min.

Rudy wrapped Jacques in the blanket he had slept on since he was a puppy and carried him to the car. He held Jacques while Min drove, and he never stopped stroking his ears. "I love his ears," he said to Min.

There wasn't much to be done at the vet's office. The doctor greeted Rudy and Min at the door, took Jacques, blanket and all, from Rudy, and laid him on an examining table.

"When did it happen?" she asked.

"Less than an hour ago. We'd been out in the yard

and he seemed happy, and then we came inside and a little while later I found him lying on the floor."

"I can assure you it was painless," said the vet.

"I wish I'd been there with him at the very . . . the very moment," said Rudy.

Min reached for Rudy's hand. "Maybe he wanted to spare you."

"Maybe." Mr. Pennington turned to the doctor. "What's to be done now?" he asked.

"We can have him cremated, if you like. We'll have his ashes ready for you in a couple of weeks."

"All right," replied Mr. Pennington.

"I'm very sorry for your loss," said the vet. "Jacques was a wonderful dog. He was a favorite here in the office."

Mr. Pennington smiled. "Thank you. I appreciate your coming in today."

When Min turned onto Aiken Avenue a few minutes later, she said, "Would you like me to come inside with you?"

"No. Thank you. I need to do this on my own."

And Mr. Pennington walked into his empty house.

CHAPTER 8

Mr. Barnes

On Monday afternoon, Flora found herself alone. Ordinarily, she walked home from school with Olivia and occasionally with Nikki, if Nikki had permission to stay in town for a couple of hours. But today Flora was on her own. And when she reached home she was still on her own, since Ruby was attending a rehearsal of the Children's Chorus.

"Hi, King. Hi, Daisy," said Flora when the cat and dog greeted her at the door. "I guess it's just us this afternoon." Flora let Daisy out into the backyard. She thought about Janie. She fixed herself a piece of toast. She thought about Janie some more. She glanced at her homework assignments and did a bit of calculating in her head. She figured she could finish the assignments by bedtime if she started them the second dinner was over.

"Yes!" she exclaimed aloud.

Flora let Daisy back inside. "Change of plans," she announced. "Sorry, but you and King are on your own after all. I'm going to go to Aunt Allie's." She picked up the phone and dialed Needle and Thread. "Min?" she said. "I decided to go to Aunt Allie's, so that's where I'll be this afternoon."

"That's fine. Did you ask Allie if it's all right with her?"

"No, but I know she needs me. She said she has to catch up with her work."

"Okay. Be home by six."

Flora hopped on her bicycle and pedaled down Aiken Avenue. On either side of her, the trees seemed to rush by, bare branches reaching into the sunshine. She flew past withered ivy vines and empty garden plots and didn't know whether to wish that winter would finally arrive or that spring would hurry up and make an early appearance.

When Flora turned into Aunt Allie's driveway, she was grateful to see that the car was in the garage. She left her bike on its side by the front walk and rang the doorbell.

"Flora!" said Allie a few moments later. "I wasn't expecting you this afternoon." Allie was holding a squirming Janie in one arm and a notebook in the other.

"I thought you might like some help."

There was just the briefest pause before Allie said, "Thank you. I could use a hand this afternoon."

"Great. That's what I'm here for." Flora stepped inside and took the baby from her aunt. "Hi, Janie. Hi,

Janie," she cooed. "Okay, Aunt Allie, you just go on and get some work done."

Allie disappeared into her study, and Flora sat on the couch in the living room with Janie. She stroked her soft curls and touched the tip of her nose. "You are so, so, so, so, so cute," she whispered. "Let's see. Do you need your diaper changed? Yes! You do. Let's go upstairs."

Flora and Ruby and Min had helped Allie to decorate Janie's nursery, and now Flora looked around it with satisfaction. She had made several of the things in the room — a pink cushion for the rocking chair and, with Min, curtains and a matching crib set. Soon Flora would finish the quilt.

"Then I think I'll start on some more rompers for you," she told her cousin.

She changed Janie's diaper, marveling at her own expertise. "And now let's find you a new outfit." Janie was wearing a purple jumper and a white T-shirt, both of which were clean, but Flora felt the need to change the outfit anyway. "Here we go," she said as she guided Janie's arms through the sleeves of a striped onesie. "Perfect."

To Flora's delight, Janie was wide-awake and happy, so she carried her downstairs and laid her on a blanket on the living room floor. "Look at all your toys. And your books! Here. I'll read to you."

Janie lay on her back and waved her arms in the air while Flora read *The Snowy Day* to her. "One day you'll see snow for yourself," Flora said. "Of course, we need cold weather for that, but we'll get some eventually."

Flora was telling Janie about snowstorms and snow days when she realized that her cousin had fallen asleep. With a sigh she carried her back upstairs and laid her in the crib. She tiptoed out of the room and down to Allie's study, where she peeked around the door. Her aunt was sitting in front of her laptop, typing furiously.

"Aunt Allie?" said Flora, and Allie jumped. "Sorry. Am I interrupting?"

"You startled me. But I'm awfully grateful to be able to get some work done. This is wonderful, Flora. Thank you. What are you and Janie up to?"

"She just went down for a nap," Flora reported. "So I was wondering what you wanted me to do now."

Allie sat back in her desk chair. "Let me see. I'm not sure."

"Do you want me to take care of Janie's laundry again?"

"Do you really want to? You could go home if you like. I'll probably have close to an hour of writing time before she wakes up."

"No, no, I'll stay!" Flora insisted.

"Well . . ."

Aunt Allie glanced surreptitiously at her watch, and Flora caught the small motion.

"I know, I know," said Flora. "You have limited time. That's why I'm going to stay to help. Won't it be nice if I get things done for you now, and then you won't have to worry about them later?"

"Yes," replied Allie, but she let a small sigh escape.

Flora clapped her hands together briskly, the way Min sometimes did. "Okay. So, what needs doing? Should I organize Janie's books? I noticed that they're a little out of order."

"Really?" murmured Aunt Allie, whose eyes were on the computer screen. She turned back to Flora. "Sorry. What did you say? Janie's books are out of order?"

"Yes. I mean, they're all just tossed randomly into her bookcase. I could straighten them out — and put them in alphabetical order."

"If you really want to, okay. But do you think you can do that without waking Janie?"

"Yes. And if I can't, I'll come back downstairs and see what else needs to be done."

"Mmm," said Allie, who was once again gazing at the screen.

Flora tiptoed back up to Janie's room. She eased the door open and settled herself in front of the bookcase. The case was low, with just two shelves, and on the top sat a lamp and several toys. Flora placed the toys in Janie's toy basket and then kneeled on the floor in front of the books. Gingerly, she slid a stack of books into her lap, immediately checking to see whether this had wakened Janie. It hadn't. She was slumbering peacefully. Flora silently emptied both shelves, divided

Janie's reading material into picture books and board books, then put the books into alphabetical order according to the author's last name, and finally slid each one tidily back onto the shelves.

There. A good job well done.

And Janie's nap was in full swing.

Flora slipped back into Allie's study. "Finished!" she announced.

Allie turned slowly from the screen. "What?" she said. "I mean, excuse me?"

"I guess you're in the middle of something, aren't you?"

Allie nodded vaguely.

"Well, the books are done. And Janie's still asleep."

"Flora, really, you've been a huge help this afternoon, and I can't tell you how much I appreciate it. But why don't you go home now? I hate to think of you hanging around here when things are so quiet. I don't —"

Flora cocked her head. "Did you hear that?"

Allie switched on the baby monitor that sat atop a filing cabinet. A whimper, rather cranky sounding, filled the study.

"She's up!" exclaimed Flora. "I'll take care of her! You go back to work, Allie. I have everything under control."

Flora dashed upstairs again and made a beeline for Janie's crib. "There you are, sleepyhead!" she said softly. "Did you have a good nap? I'd better check your diaper again."

Flora spent the next few minutes once again changing Janie's diaper and then unnecessarily changing her outfit, too.

"You are the cutest, cutest, cutest girl in all of Camden Falls!" announced Flora, hoisting her cousin in the air. "Let me get you a bottle, and then maybe we can go for a walk outside, since it's so warm."

After Janie had been fed (expertly, in Flora's opinion), Flora poked her head into Allie's study. "Here she is, all dressed and fed and ready to go outside. It's pretty warm today. We could take a nice long walk."

"That's a good idea," replied Allie, and she helped Flora settle Janie in a nest of blankets in her fancy new stroller.

"We'll see you later," called Flora as she wheeled Janie down the driveway to the sidewalk.

Allie's neighborhood was bustling. The streets here were lined not with the large and aging homes of Flora's neighborhood but with smaller, newer houses, and in the yards of most of them were bicycles and tricycles and ride-on toys, basketball nets and skateboards and plastic slides. Flora saw kids playing and dogs being walked and a group of boys heading somewhere with a bat and ball.

"Maybe," said Flora to Janie, "there are other babies in these houses, and one day they'll be your friends. You and your friends will grow up together and go to Camden Falls Elementary, just like Ruby and I did. And you —"

Flora stopped talking when she heard someone call her name.

"Flora? Is that you?"

Flora had wheeled Janie two blocks in one direction, turned around and gone three blocks back in the other direction, and now had turned around a second time and was approaching Allie's driveway. She looked over her shoulder.

Climbing out of his car in the driveway of the house across the street was her English teacher, Mr. Barnes. He waved to her.

Flora waved back. Then, feeling both proud and shy, she wheeled Janie up her teacher's driveway. "Have you met my new cousin?" she asked.

"Not officially," replied Mr. Barnes. He set his briefcase at his feet.

"This is Janie," Flora told him. "Jane Marie Read. She's named for my sister and me. Those are our middle names. My aunt adopted her last month. I mean, that's when it became official. But Janie was born on Thanksgiving Day."

Mr. Barnes peeked into the stroller and Janie waved her arms at him. He smiled. Then he cleared his throat. "So . . . your aunt adopted her?"

"All by herself," said Flora proudly.

Mr. Barnes glanced thoughtfully across the street. "That was very brave of her."

"She really, really wanted a baby. And," Flora continued, inspired, "there was no —" She paused, searching for the right phrase. "There was no man on the horizon."

Mr. Barnes reddened. And in a flash, Flora saw it all: Her teacher had a crush on her aunt. He had barely spoken two words to her since he'd moved in at the beginning of the school year, but he was in luv with Aunt Allie.

What if, Flora wondered with a rush of excitement, Mr. Barnes and Aunt Allie got married? It would be perfect. The English teacher married to the writer. Aunt Allie would get a husband, Janie would get a father, and Mr. Barnes would get a whole family.

CHAPTER 9

Ruby the Perfect

Ruby stood outside the window of Heaven, the jewelry store. Well, the old jewelry store, thought Ruby. A newer and much fancier one had opened in Camden Falls recently, but Ruby was desperately hoping that she might find a replacement owl here at Heaven, where things were cheaper. Heaven was where Ruby had bought plastic rings and rubber bracelets, sparkly hair combs and once a silver seagull, a birthday present for Min. Except that it wasn't silver, as it had turned out. It was pewter, which Flora said Ruby should have known by the price: $11.49. And also by the fact that the tag was stuck to the bottom of the gull. A silver gull of that size would have been hideously expensive, according to know-it-all Flora, and would never have had anything stuck to its bottom. The tag would have been tastefully arranged (facedown) *next* to the gull. Ruby had never spent more than the $11.49 on any one item at Heaven. So she was keeping her fingers crossed that in the display in the window or in one of the cases inside the store she might find an owl that looked like the one she had broken. Even a glass owl would be fine. Ruby didn't care. Glass, crystal. Would Min really know the difference?

Ruby blew on her bare hands as she scanned the earrings and necklaces and watches in the window. She realized her hands were freezing and felt in her pockets for mittens. But her pockets were bare. The winter had been so warm that Ruby had rarely needed either mittens or a hat. She found herself wishing for both now.

Ruby saw nothing resembling a crystal owl in the window, so she stepped inside and began a careful examination of each display case. It was while she was standing in front of a rack of silver (well, pewter) earrings and wondering if she might have enough money for an owl *and* a pair of earrings in the shape of ballet slippers that she became aware of the radio playing somewhere in the store. And then she realized what single word had just captured her attention: *blizzard*.

"What?" said Ruby aloud. She stepped back and stood in the aisle, listening intently.

"That's right, ladies and gentlemen," the announcer was saying, and Ruby detected a hint of excitement in his usually calm voice. "A blizzard. All of our computer models are predicting that it will arrive late Friday afternoon. We're expecting high winds, temperatures well below freezing, and — good news for the kiddies — more than two feet of snow. Yup, twenty-four to thirty inches of the white stuff. This could be the worst storm in forty years."

Now, ordinarily if Ruby had heard such an announcement, particularly in a winter that so far had yielded a scant flurry here and there, she might have jumped up and down and cheered, even in the middle of Heaven. But at the moment, all she could think was: Friday. The weather guy said the storm is supposed to come on *Friday*. Friday *afternoon*, no less. There was no way they would get a snow day out of the blizzard, even the worst one in forty years, if it began late on Friday afternoon.

"Ruby? What's wrong?"

Ruby jumped and returned her attention to the jewelry case, where, she now saw, Margaret Malone was standing. She had forgotten that Margaret worked at Heaven. She'd started her new job after the holidays in order to earn money for college.

"Did you hear that?" asked Ruby.

"Hear what?"

"What the weatherman just said. A blizzard is coming on Friday. *Friday*. We won't get a snow day. All that snow, and what good will it do?"

Margaret laughed. "Well, it should be exciting. And fun. Aren't you excited, even a little?"

"I guess," replied Ruby. She scanned the display cases again.

"Are you looking for anything special?"

"Well . . ." Ruby hesitated. Should she mention the owl to Margaret? She didn't want Min to hear that she was going around town looking for a crystal owl. On the other hand, if she could find a cheap owl here, it *would* make things much easier. "I don't suppose you have any owls," said Ruby finally.

"Any owls?"

"I'm looking for a crystal owl. It's, um, a present for someone."

Margaret shook her head. "We don't have anything like that."

"A glass owl would do."

But Margaret shook her head again. "Sorry."

"Well, okay. Thanks anyway," said Ruby.

Outside, she stuffed her hands in her pockets. Only Tuesday afternoon and already she could feel a change in the weather. The sun was shining and the storm was still three days away, but the air was certainly colder. Ruby blew out her breath and watched with satisfaction as it puffed in front of her.

She paused and looked up and down Main Street. Okay. Where else might she find an owl for Min? Ruby looked in Bubble Gum, where she found a tiny china owl, and in Stuff 'n' Nonsense, where she found another china owl, and in two other stores, where she didn't find any owls at all. That left Whitworth Jewelers, the new jewelry store — which was also the expensive jewelry store.

"Rats," said Ruby as she stepped inside.

"May I help you?" someone asked her before she even had time to close the door all the way.

"Me?" said Ruby.

A man was standing behind the longest of three counters in the store. He was wearing a suit and tie, and he was peering at her over a pair of reading glasses. Something in his voice made Ruby suspect that he might be foreign, possibly British. Now he glanced around the store, which was empty except for another salesperson, as if to say, "Do you see anyone else who needs help?" But he said nothing, simply steepled his fingers and continued to stare at her.

"Well," said Ruby, taking in the immaculate store, the thick carpet, the jewelry arranged on pillows of black velvet, "I'm looking for a . . . a crystal owl." She had almost said "glass owl" but caught herself in time. Nothing in Whitworth Jewelers would be created from something as lowly as glass.

"All of our crystal is in this case," said the man, and he walked to the back of the store. "We have several crystal animals, and we do in fact have an owl."

"You do?! You have an owl?" Ruby clapped her hands together. "That's great."

"There it is," said the man, pointing.

Ruby saw a crystal owl that was beautiful, but not exactly like the one she'd broken. It was larger, and its wings were in a different position.

"Is — is that the only one you have?"

The man cleared his throat. "Yes."

Ruby paused. "How much is it?" she dared to ask.

The man told her the price and Ruby swallowed hard. She would have to work for months in order to earn enough money to buy it. She was about to ask if she could buy the owl on time, or if it could be set aside and put on hold for her for until April, but the man was still glaring at her, and Ruby's mouth suddenly felt dry. At last she said, "Well, thank you. It's really nice, but I guess I won't buy it right now."

She turned and fled from the store. Outside, she stood in the sunshine and drew in a few deep breaths. Okay. She couldn't afford the owl just yet, but at least she knew where to find an owl that looked reasonably like the one she'd broken, and she knew how much money she'd need to earn as the Doer of Unpleasant Jobs in order to buy it. It was a beginning. Ruby had a goal.

Ruby ran all the way back to the Row Houses that afternoon, and the moment she was safely in her room she withdrew her personal and private self-improvement plan from her desk drawer and studied it.

1. Be neater.

Ruby grinned and silently congratulated herself. She was already neater. She had kept her room and her desk tidy since the moment she had drawn up the plan. Just that morning Min had poked her head into Ruby's room and said, "My land." Usually this was followed by, "Did something explode in here?" But this time she'd exclaimed, "I'd hardly know this was your room, Ruby. I can see the floor." Then she'd smiled and added, "Good for you, honey. I really appreciate this. You should be very proud of yourself."

2. *Go to all lessons and rehearsals unless I am sick.*

Well, she hadn't had too many lessons and rehearsals in the past few days, but she hadn't missed any of them, so that was good.

Ruby skimmed the rest of the list. She was working as hard as she could. She was trying to be polite and not sarcastic, to plan ahead, to think before she acted, blah, blah, blah. Frankly, it was a little tedious. But Ruby did enjoy the compliments she was getting. She had handed all her homework in on time since making her list, and her teacher had noticed.

"Ruby, I'm impressed," she'd said, smiling, on Monday morning when Ruby had handed in her weekend homework. "I didn't need to give you any reminders."

Thinking about this, Ruby allowed a smile to spread across her face.

"Ruby!" called Flora from downstairs. "Phone for you!"

"I'll take it in Min's room!" Ruby called back.

She ran down the hall and picked up the extension by Min's bed. "Hello?"

"Hello, Ruby? This is Rudy Pennington. Are you available to do some work over the weekend?"

"Sure," said Ruby.

"I just heard about the storm and I was wondering if you'd be able to help me with shoveling."

"Definitely," replied Ruby. She carried the phone into her bedroom and found a pad of paper. "Let me write this down. We can figure out when you want me to come after we see how bad the storm is."

"Very businesslike of you," commented Mr. Pennington.

"Thank you," replied Ruby. She had just hung up the phone when it rang again. "Hello?"

"Hi, Ruby. This is Dr. Malone. Would you be able to take care of Twinkle and Bandit when we go away in a couple of weeks?"

"Of course," said Ruby, who was already reaching for her pad.

At dinnertime, her homework finished and a third job lined up, Ruby joined Min and Flora in the kitchen.

"If it's all right with you, I'm going to practice for tap class after dinner," she announced. Before Min could say anything, Ruby added, "My homework is done. You can check it if you want. Oh, and I started my book report, but it isn't due until Friday, so I have plenty of time to finish it."

She looked with satisfaction at her sister and her grandmother, both of whom had stopped what they were doing and were actually staring at Ruby. She smiled at them and began to set the table.

CHAPTER 10

Olivia the Moody

Olivia was moody. *Moody* wasn't a word with which she was very familiar, but if it meant that her moods swung back and forth for no reason at all, and that she felt crabby and wanted to be alone more often than she felt content and friendly, and that she was often tempted to slam her bedroom door — preferably in someone's face — well, then, *moody* described perfectly the way she'd been feeling lately.

She had heard her parents talking about her one evening when they thought she'd gone to sleep.

"Olivia's been awfully moody lately," her father had said.

"Moody isn't the word," her mother had replied, and Olivia had thought, It's exactly the word. *Exactly.* And she'd felt unreasonably annoyed when her mother had laughed then, even if she had laughed fondly.

A moment later her mother had said something about hormones and teenagers, but Olivia, who was standing at the top of the stairs, trying to hear a conversation taking place on the first floor, couldn't quite catch the rest of what was said.

She supposed she should have been happy to hear anything about herself connected with the word *teenagers*, since Olivia longed to be older, taller, more shapely, more worldly, all those elusive teenage things. But when her mother used *Olivia*, *teenagers*, and *hormones* in the same sentence and then laughed, fondly or otherwise, Olivia felt only the desire to slam her bedroom door.

She didn't slam it. But she did stalk back to her room, climb into her bed, and lie there miserably, thinking dark thoughts about boys in general, Jacob in particular, Melody and Tanya, and even Flora and Nikki. She wondered if, next door, Flora was still awake, maybe sitting at her desk, finishing her homework. It was Wednesday night, and Flora had said on the way home from school that she had so much homework she wouldn't be able to spend time with Janie that afternoon.

Olivia placed her ear to her wall and listened for sounds from Ruby's bedroom. She thought that if Ruby was up, that might mean Flora was up as well. But she heard nothing.

Olivia flopped onto her bed again. She still hadn't told Flora or Nikki about her date with Jacob, at least not the truth about the date. She had said, "It was fun," and, "The movie was great." But what she longed to say was, "It was horrible. Melody and Tanya were sitting right behind us, but that wasn't the worst thing. The worst thing was that Jacob held my hand during the show. The *entire* show. His hand was sweaty, and I couldn't concentrate on the movie, and he was just trying to be nice to me, but all I wanted was to get away from him. What's *wrong* with me?"

She imagined Flora saying, "I don't know what's wrong with you. Why was holding Jacob's hand worse than sitting in front of Melody and Tanya for two hours?"

Of course, that wasn't really what Flora would say. But it was what Olivia had been thinking for four days.

Maybe that's why I'm so moody, thought Olivia. I'm being awfully mean to myself.

Olivia lay in her bed, feeling as if she didn't belong in her own body. As if she'd gotten too big for it, or it had gotten too big for her, or maybe she was in someone else's body altogether. She didn't fall asleep until long after her parents had tiptoed upstairs and turned out their light.

The next morning, to her surprise, considering the small amount of sleep she'd had, not to mention her dark mood of the night before, she awoke feeling rather cheerful. And as she and Flora walked to school, she made a decision. Today, no matter what, she was going to tell Jacob that she and Flora and Nikki needed to eat lunch alone. They needed to talk. Nikki, Olivia knew, needed moral support from her friends. And Olivia could have used a little herself. At the very least, she wanted to tell them how she was feeling about Jacob.

Olivia's good mood lasted through the morning, and at lunchtime she marched resolutely into the cafeteria, determined to tell Jacob that she couldn't sit with him, but that she'd call him that evening. She picked out her lunch, paid for it, and carried it to the table by the windows, where Nikki and Flora were just settling in with their own lunches. Jacob wasn't there yet, which was fine. Olivia could snag him before he sat down. She turned, scanned the cafeteria for Jacob but couldn't find him, and when she turned back to the table, Melody and Tanya were there. Two seconds later, Jacob had joined them.

Olivia sagged. She couldn't leave Jacob with Melody and Tanya. That would be like leaving a baby bunny with two hungry foxes.

Olivia, Jacob, Melody, and Tanya all sat down at once, Jacob sliding into the seat to the right of Olivia, the hungry foxes directly across the table.

Olivia glanced at Flora, who was sitting on her left. Flora was looking back at her with wide eyes, brows raised, as if to say, "How did *this* happen?"

Olivia shook her head. What on earth were Melody and Tanya doing, getting in such close range of Jacob? Were they going to snag him right in front of her?

"Hey, Olivia," said Melody.

"Hey, Olivia," said Tanya.

Olivia unwrapped her sandwich and half of it fell apart, tomato slices sliding across the tray. "Hey," she replied.

"So, what do you have going for the weekend?" Tanya asked.

Olivia, attempting to reconstruct the sandwich, detected an awkward silence. She glanced up. Everyone was looking at her. "Who, me?" she said.

Tanya smiled sweetly at her. "Yeah. Any plans?"

Olivia cleared her throat. "Well, the blizzard . . ."

"Oh, that's right. The storm," said Melody. "I can't wait. I love big storms."

"So do I," Olivia replied cautiously.

"Really? You like storms, too?"

"Well, sure."

Tanya crunched on a carrot stick. "What's your favorite thing about a storm?"

Olivia squirmed. Was this a trick of some kind? Melody and Tanya usually discussed clothes and boys and ways to get to the mall without their parents.

"Um," said Olivia, "I don't know." What was the right answer? Surely not sledding with her brothers. Or making paper dolls with Flora, which they had done twice the winter before. "No school?" she said finally, as if she'd been called on in class and had to guess at the answer.

Tanya grinned at her. "Yeah, a snow day is the best."

"We're not going to get a snow day out of this storm, though," Jacob spoke up, just as Olivia was thinking that this had to be the lamest conversation ever. She continued to wait for a trap to reveal itself, one she would step in spectacularly — saying some-thing that would cause her to hang her head, cheeks burning with embarrassment.

"Oh, well," said Melody. "I don't care if we don't get a snow day. I like just lying in bed on a snowy morning, looking at how the light in my room is different, kind of silvery. You can always tell when it's snowing. Even when the blinds are down you can tell."

Olivia said nothing and eventually realized that Melody and Tanya were watching her again. But they appeared friendly enough.

Something was expected of Olivia here. She was supposed to say something. Anything.

"One of my favorite books in first grade," said Olivia, "was *Snowbound With Betsy*. It was about this little girl, Betsy, and her sister Star, and they get snow-bound the week before Christmas. . . ."

Uh-oh. This was it. The trap. Olivia had just men-tioned the most uncool and babyish thing possible.

She glanced across the table and saw that, sure enough, Melody and Tanya were gaping at her. Tanya's mouth was actually open.

"I mean . . ." mumbled Olivia, who had no idea what to say next.

But Melody brightened. "Yeah, I used to like that book, too."

Tanya swallowed a bite of her sandwich and said, "So who's going to the game next week?"

What game? thought Olivia.

"I am," said Jacob.

"Cool," said Tanya. "We'll see you there."

Apparently, there was to be a basketball game on Wednesday. Olivia wasn't sure who was playing. Two Central teams? Central against someone else? But Jacob was going and so were Tanya and Melody, and as they talked about it, a thought came to Olivia that made her feel chilled all over. What if she and Jacob broke up but remained friends, and then Jacob started going out with Tanya or Melody? How could Olivia stand that? The answer was that she wouldn't be able to stand it. And that would be the end of her friendship with Jacob. She didn't want Jacob for her boyfriend, but she definitely wanted him for her friend, and she realized now that she could never be like — who was that star? Bruce Willis. That was it. Bruce had continued to hang around with his former wife even after she started going out with another guy. Olivia couldn't do that if Jacob's next girlfriend was Melody or Tanya.

"Hey, Olivia, you and Jacob should come with us to the game next week," Tanya said suddenly.

"We should come with you?" Olivia squeaked. She attempted to lower her voice. "Jacob and I should come with you?"

"Sure. It would be fun."

"Well . . ."

"We'll let you know later," replied Jacob. "Thanks."

• × • × •

"You guys," said Olivia to Flora and Nikki that afternoon as they headed out of school, loaded down by books, "Tanya and Melody were actually nice to me at lunch."

"What? About the game?" said Flora. "You guys aren't going to go with them, are you?"

"Well, I don't know. Why not?"

"Why not?" exclaimed Nikki. "Because . . . because Melody and Tanya remind me of my father. He's been giving all these presents to Mae for some reason. I don't know why, but there's something behind it. He's up to something. And I think Tanya is up to something, too."

"Oh, so she can't be nice to me just because she likes me? Hello, Tanya invited Jacob *and* me to the game. Together. Why do you think there's anything behind that?"

"I —" Nikki started to say.

But Olivia was already marching away from her friends. They watched her stalk out the front door of the school and across the lawn toward Main Street. By the time she reached Sincerely Yours — alone — her moodiness had returned, sprouting like a poisonous mushroom. Maddeningly, she knew that her friends were right. Melody and Tanya were up to something. And if Olivia went to the game with them, she would step directly into their trap.

CHAPTER 11

A Tree Grows in Brooklyn

Willow Hamilton deposited her groaning backpack in her locker atop a stack consisting of shoes, loose papers, and an unfinished art project. Then she withdrew a single book from the shelf. *A Tree Grows in Brooklyn*. The afternoon rush at Camden Falls Central — more harried on a Friday than on any other afternoon of the week — had ended, and the halls were growing quiet. A footfall here and there. A last-minute reminder: "Don't forget to call me after you ask your mother!" A door closing, the lock snicking into place.

Willow carried her book to the end of the hall and stood by the window. It was a tall window, stretching from the ceiling almost to the floor, and afforded Willow a view of the front lawn of the school and of the road beyond. The school buses had lined up in the lane beside the road, and now, doors closed, everyone aboard, were pulling into the traffic one by one.

She shifted her gaze to the lawn and saw a girl

running across it, her hand planted on her head to hold her hat in place. The wind was blowing ferociously. Willow could hear it whistling around the corner of the building. She glanced at the sky, which was heavy with clouds, and she shivered.

Storm coming.

It was time for the next meeting of the seventh-grade book club. Friday wasn't their usual meeting day, but it had worked for everyone this month, and Willow didn't mind staying after school for another hour on a Friday afternoon.

She looked at her watch. Ten minutes until the meeting.

Outside, branches lashed back and forth, and Willow watched one crack from its trunk and hurtle to the ground, startling a red squirrel that leaped nearly a foot in the air before scurrying across the lawn. She wondered what her mother would do during the storm, if life in the hospital would be changed by a blizzard, or if maybe her mother's routine — surely there was a routine — would march along whether the snow fell or not. She hoped her mother would enjoy the storm. Willow planned to. She and her father and brother had already talked about the weekend, and her father had bought canned soup and peanut butter and bananas, things that wouldn't spoil if the power went out. He'd bought popcorn, too. "We're going to make it the old-fashioned way," he'd said. "In the fireplace."

"You can make popcorn in the *fire*place?" Cole had asked incredulously.

"Absolutely," Mr. Hamilton had replied. "People have been eating popcorn for thousands of years. They popped it over open flames long before there were microwaves."

"What else are we going to cook in the fireplace?" Cole had wanted to know.

Mr. Hamilton had cleared his throat. "Well, I think the popcorn will be enough. But maybe we can have a picnic in the living room."

"And eat on the floor?"

"And eat on the floor."

This was exactly the kind of conversation the Hamiltons would never have been able to have before Willow's mother had gone to the hospital. Willow recalled, with a familiar lurching feeling in her stomach, the years spent with her mother, trying to understand the bewildering, ever-changing rules with which she ran their household. Not to mention the orderliness, the tidiness. Her mother would never have allowed a picnic on the living room floor.

Willow tried to focus on the weekend, which was certain to be exciting. (The biggest storm in forty years!) But her mother had found her way into her thoughts and now Willow recalled the conversation she'd had with her father the previous weekend. It had taken place on Sunday afternoon while Cole was playing outside with the Morris boys and Willow was deeply involved in *A Tree Grows in Brooklyn*, which she thought was one of the best books she had read in her entire life.

"Knock, knock," her father had said, standing in her bedroom doorway.

"You could actually knock," Willow had told him, smiling.

"I know. I guess 'knock, knock' is corny. Can we talk for a minute?"

Her father had sat on Willow's desk chair, and Willow, who had been lying on her bed, had straightened up and set the book aside. "Is something wrong?" she'd asked.

Her father had shaken his head. "No. But I promised you I'd keep you informed about your mother, and I had a conference with the doctors on Friday. I thought you'd like to know what we talked about."

Willow, who had been comfortably settled in Francie Nolan's world of Brooklyn more than a hundred years in the past, had felt her chest tighten. "Okay," she'd said. "I mean, yes, tell me what the doctors said."

"They think your mother will be ready to come home in about three months — the middle of April. She's making good progress."

Willow let her breath out but said nothing.

"Are you okay with that?" her father had asked.

"I guess I have to be."

"No, you don't. But if you aren't, we need to talk about it."

"I want her to come home. She's my mother. But . . . everything's going to change. And since she left it's been so, I don't know, so peaceful here. Cole is happier . . ."

"You're happier," Mr. Hamilton had said.

Willow had nodded. "And I can't even think about the rules, all the things she used to ask us to do. They never made sense. Cole and I couldn't keep them straight."

"But she's been working on the rules — or her need for them — while she's been in the hospital. I promise you that when she comes home, things will not be the way they were before."

"How can you promise something like that?" Willow had asked.

"Okay. Fair enough. I can't promise. But I can tell you that the doctors are very pleased with her progress. And another thing — something I actually *can* promise: I plan to be at home much more than I used to be. And you and Cole and I will talk more than we used to. Okay?"

Willow had nodded. And she had tried to feel comfortable with the new knowledge, especially since she truly did miss her mother. But when she thought about April, her stomach lurched and her chest tightened.

"Hey, Willow!"

Willow turned from the window, leaving her thoughts outside with the gathering storm, and peered down the hallway. "Hi, Olivia! Hi, Flora!"

"Ready for the meeting?" asked Olivia.

Willow held up her book. "Yup."

"Walk with us to Mr. Barnes's room," said Flora. "We're going to meet Nikki there."

It was hard to miss Mr. Barnes's classroom. It was the only one on its corridor with a small crowd of students outside the door.

"There's Nikki," said Olivia.

"Let's find seats together," said Willow.

The girls edged through the door, Flora saying, "Hey, Mr. Barnes, Aunt Allie just sold another book to her publisher. Isn't that exciting?"

This piece of information seemed to make Mr. Barnes look flustered, intrigued, and embarrassed all at once, a source of fascination for Willow, who continued to glance at him as she and her friends settled themselves in a row on the window ledge near the front of the room.

"What —" she started to ask Flora.

But at that moment Mr. Barnes clapped his hands and said, "If everyone's here we'd better get started. I'd like to send you on your way before it starts snowing. Who wants to begin?"

A forest of hands shot into the air.

"Rachel?" said Mr. Barnes.

"This was the best book I ever read in my whole life."

"Me, too," said a chorus of voices.

And Willow added, "I thought that when I'd only read a few chapters and I never changed my opinion."

"Why was it such a good book, do you think?" asked Mr. Barnes.

Another forest of hands. This time Mr. Barnes stepped back and sat on his desk, and the students knew the discussion was now up to them.

"You get pulled right into Francie's world," said a girl.

"But it isn't a very nice world," said Jacob, who had rushed into the room at the last minute and plopped down next to Olivia. "I mean, Francie's family hardly has any money, they don't have enough to eat, her father drinks — and still you want to keep reading on and on about the Nolans."

"Because you like Francie so much," said Flora.

"Because Francie's mother has so much hope," said Nikki.

"Because her world is so different from ours," said someone else. "Imagine looking out the back window of your apartment and seeing a man taking care of a horse in the yard of *his* apartment building. And the kids had a lot of freedom. Even little kids. They collected stuff and got to sell it and keep the money and spend it on candy. All on their own. No adults around."

"Penny candy actually cost a penny."

"Deliveries were made by horse and buggy."

"Francie's mother could make a meal for the whole family out of stale bread and an onion and a tiny bit of meat."

"I liked the story because it was about Francie but it was about other people in her life, too, including grown-ups," spoke up Nikki. "It wasn't really a kids' book."

"Some things made me uncomfortable," said Claudette Tisch. "The way Francie and her family talked about people who were Jewish or Italian. I didn't like the names they used."

"But I guess that's the way things were in a neighborhood like Francie's back then," said Willow. "That's how people really talked. If the author hadn't used those names, the story wouldn't have been . . . what's the word? Authentic?"

The conversation continued, but Willow noticed that Mr. Barnes glanced out the window more and more often until finally he said, "I'm sorry to interrupt, kids, but I'm getting a little concerned about the weather. I think we should wrap things up a bit early and get you on your way home."

Ten minutes later, the members of the club had chosen the book for their next meeting and were gathering their belongings and emptying into the hallway.

"Bye, Mr. Barnes," said Flora as she breezed by his desk. "I'll tell Aunt Allie hello for you."

Willow looked curiously at Flora but held her tongue until she and Flora and Olivia and Nikki were leaving the school grounds and heading for Main Street. At last she said, "Flora? If you don't mind my asking, how come you kept mentioning your aunt to Mr. Barnes?"

Flora let a slow smile spread across her face. "I think Mr. Barnes has a crush on her," she said.

Well. That's interesting, thought Willow. You just never know what's around the corner. She thought about Francie Nolan, who had started her story mired in poverty and managed to rise above it. Maybe, Willow realized, her mother's return would yield surprises.

Willow tipped her head up to the clouds, squeezed her eyes shut, and made a wish for her family.

CHAPTER 12

Blizzard

"It's here! It's here!" cried Mae. She turned from the window. "Come on, everyone! Come look outside. You can see snow in the light from the porch."

Nikki, Tobias, and Mrs. Sherman joined Mae at the window. Sure enough, the snow had begun to fall, and not just a flake here and there, but fistfuls of snow being hurled from the sky. The storm had held off all afternoon, and Nikki, despite the dire predictions on every single television news show, had begun to think that maybe the blizzard wouldn't hit Camden Falls after all. But here it was.

"It's snowing pretty hard, considering it just began," commented Tobias.

"I think we're as prepared as we can be," said Mrs. Sherman. "We have plenty of food in case we can't get to the store for a few days and plenty of firewood in case the electricity goes off. And I don't have to go into work until Monday."

"I left food in one of the sheds for the dogs," added Nikki, "if they can make their way to it. Where do you think stray dogs go during a big storm?"

"Honey, don't worry about that," said her mother.

"I can't help it. Paw-Paw could be one of them. He *was* one of them."

"But he's here with us now, and you've done all you can for the others. I think they'll find shelter before the snow gets too deep."

"How much snow is twenty-four to thirty inches?" asked Mae. "That's what the weatherman keeps saying we're going to get."

"Two to two and a half feet," Tobias told her. "That's about up to there on you," he added, pointing to her waist.

"Whoa," whispered Mae. "I couldn't even *walk* through snow that deep." She paused. "Think of the giant snowmen we can make. Hey, how are we even going to be able to open the front door tomorrow?"

"It might be hard," admitted Tobias. "I'm glad I'm here to help you guys with the shoveling."

"This is the most exciting thing that has ever happened to me," Mae declared dramatically. "I don't know *how* I'm going to be able to eat my dinner."

"You'd better eat it, though," said her mother. "It might be the last hot meal you get for a couple of days."

"I hope the power does go out!" Mae skipped to the table and slid into her seat. "It would be an adventure."

Apparently, Mae didn't remember the days when the Shermans' power was regularly cut off because they hadn't paid their bills.

By the time dinner was over, more than an inch of snow had fallen. Nikki watched as her sister flitted back and forth between the window and the array of toys her father had been bringing her. Every time he showed up at the Shermans' house he brought something else for Mae and occasionally something for Nikki or Tobias. But Mae's treasure was piling up faster than the snow. A board game, art supplies, a pair of cowgirl boots, clothes for her new doll. The gift he'd arrived with the previous afternoon, though, had topped all the others: a completely furnished dollhouse. And not a gaudy plastic dollhouse with stiff plastic dolls and pink plastic furniture, but a large wooden house with a front that opened to reveal the rooms inside, furnished with intricate dressers and tables and beds and chairs and couches — all considerably fancier than anything human-size that the Shermans owned.

Mae kneeled before the house, opened its front, and gazed at the rooms inside. "Dining room," she said dreamily, "kitchen, bedrooms, playroom, living room."

"In a house that fancy," said Tobias, "I think you call the living room the parlor."

Mae continued to stare at her treasure. "I'm going to switch everything around," she said. "I'm going to put the bedrooms downstairs and the kitchen upstairs and — hey, this house doesn't have a bathroom!"

"You could turn that room into the bathroom," said Nikki, squatting beside her sister and pointing to the second floor.

"But there's no furniture for a bathroom."

"We'll make the furniture. That's the fun of a dollhouse."

"I am not," said Mae indignantly, "going to make a toilet." She examined the dolls — a girl, a boy, a mother, and a father — that had come with the set. "But you know what we could do tomorrow when we're snowed in? We could make some more clothes for the dolls. Boy, Nikki, this is the best present I ever got. Daddy is so nice."

Nikki smiled at her sister, but as she stood up she felt an uncomfortably familiar sensation wash over her — a feeling of the world tilting or of the need to swerve out of the path of danger — and a phrase wormed its way into her head: *Something wicked this way comes.*

"Mom?" said Nikki. "Can we talk?"

"Of course," replied her mother, who was curled up on one end of the couch.

"I mean, in my room? Now?"

"Oh." Mrs. Sherman set her magazine aside. "Nikki? Are you all right?"

Nikki nodded, but she frowned as she looked at her sister, who was busily removing furniture from the dollhouse. She led the way to the second floor, the words *Something wicked this way comes* sounding in her head like a drumbeat in time to her footsteps, and closed the door behind her mother.

"I'm scared," said Nikki. She threw herself onto her bed and hugged a pillow to her chest.

"What's the matter?" Mrs. Sherman sat on Nikki's desk chair and leaned forward, hands clasped in front of her.

"I was watching Mae play with the dollhouse," Nikki began, and then her words slid away from her. "All the presents . . ." She drew in a breath and started over for a second time. "Mae said this morning that she wants to visit Dad this summer. I think she meant that she wants to go to South Carolina."

"But I'll have full custody —"

"I hate him! I hate that he's doing this! He's *bribing* her. And why? What does he hope will happen? And why isn't he trying to bribe Tobias and me?"

"Honey, your father is complicated."

"No, he's not. He's mean."

"He's complicated. People are complicated, and a divorce is complicated."

"He's trying to make Mae change her mind so that she'll want to live with him."

"I don't think so," said Mrs. Sherman. "And in any case, that can't happen. We've been through this, honey. Your father isn't in a position to have any of you kids live with him."

"Then why is he bribing Mae?"

"I don't know that he's bribing her. Maybe he just wants her to think of him as a good father."

"Being a good father isn't about presents! Dad's taking the easy way out."

"You know that, and I know that —"

"But Mae doesn't."

"I think," said Mrs. Sherman, "that because your father is aware of how you and Tobias feel about him, he'd like for Mae to feel differently."

Nikki fell silent.

Her mother stood up, stretched, and joined her on the bed. "I'm not saying that what your father is doing is right, but I think that what he's doing is human. Nikki, nothing is going to come of the gifts —"

"You mean the bribery."

"— so why don't you stop worrying? Let Mae enjoy the presents. She's not going to go live in South Carolina."

"Are you *sure* you'll have full custody?" asked Nikki. "Are you absolutely positive?"

"I am absolutely positive. The paperwork has been under way for quite some time. It's true that it hasn't been finalized yet, but your father has never asked for full custody, and he can't afford to have you and Mae live with him. It simply isn't going to happen. It has never even been an issue."

"The presents are making me nervous."

"They shouldn't be. I promise you that they aren't going to change a thing."

That night, Mae couldn't sleep. Every couple of hours she woke up, pulled aside the curtains, and tried to see whether the snow was still falling. "Nikki," she would call across the room, "I think maybe the snow is twelve inches high now." Or, "Nikki, I can't see anything. It's too dark! Is it still snowing?"

Finally, Nikki got up, tiptoed downstairs in the chilly house, and turned on the light over the back stoop. "Now," she said to Mae as she scooted into her bed again, "you'll be able to see the snow all night long. Only please don't wake me up again, okay?"

"Okay."

Nikki closed her eyes.

"Nikki? When is it supposed to stop snowing?"

"I don't know."

"Tonight?"

"I don't know."

"Tomorrow?"

"Maybe. I think so."

"Nikki?"

"WHAT?"

"What do you think it feels like when the snow is as high as your waist?"

"You'll have to find out tomorrow. After you've had a good night's sleep."

Mae sighed and then looked out the window again. "Hey, the light works really well! I can see the snow flying through the air, flying on a dare, flying without a care. Hey, Nikki, I should write a poem about the snow."

"Great. Write it silently in your head now, and tomorrow you can put it on paper."

"Okay. Nikki? Is there snow in South Carolina?"

"Not a flake."

"Really? Daddy will never see snow?"

"I'm not sure. I'll help you look it up tomorrow, but only if you go to sleep right now."

The next morning, Nikki made her way groggily to the kitchen at nearly nine o'clock. The snow was falling thickly, and Tobias, who had slept soundly all night, was struggling with the front door. At last he said, "I guess there's really no point in opening this until the storm is over."

"How much snow do you think we have so far?" Nikki wanted to know. "I'm only asking so that you'll be prepared for Mae's questions."

"Hey, is she still asleep?"

"Yes, and whatever you do, don't wake her up. You'll be sorry."

Tobias grinned.

Mrs. Sherman, who was watching the Weather Channel in the living room, called, "Sure enough, the worst storm in forty years!"

Nikki opened the refrigerator and pulled out a loaf of bread. "Tobias, do you think I can get out to the shed to see if the dogs found the food?"

"What, now? No way. Seriously, I can't open the door."

And at that moment, the power went out. The television turned off with an odd chirp, the lights flickered and disappeared, the refrigerator stopped humming, the voice on the kitchen radio faded away, and the toaster, which had just started to glow red, faded to pink and gray and finally black.

"Well, Mae will be happy," said Tobias.

"Why?" asked Mae, running down the stairs in her nightgown.

"The power just went out," replied Mrs. Sherman.

"Goody! Can we eat everything in the refrigerator? Can I have ice cream for breakfast?"

Mrs. Sherman hesitated and then smiled. "Yes," she said. "You may have ice cream for breakfast."

Nikki turned her thoughts away from South Carolina and dollhouses and stray dogs. She put the loaf of bread back in the refrigerator. "You know what?" she said. "I'm going to have ice cream for breakfast, too." And she and Mae sat at the table with dishes of Cherry Garcia before them and watched the snow swirl outside the windows.

CHAPTER 13

Spill the Beans

"Hey!" cried Jack Walter, flicking the kitchen light switch up and down. "The electricity's off!"

Olivia, who had just woken up and had followed her brother down the stairs, looked at a stopped clock in the living room and paused, listening.

"Nothing," she said.

"What?" asked Henry, and he jumped down the last four steps, landing behind her.

"I don't hear a single sound except our voices. No TV, no radio, nothing humming. Nothing."

"Mom!" called Henry. "Dad! The power's out!"

"It went out a little while ago," replied Mrs. Walter. She and Olivia's father were sitting at the table in the dining room, trying to read the previous day's newspaper by the gray light from the windows.

"Whoa, look at all that snow!" exclaimed Jack, and Olivia and Henry joined him at the back door.

"Eighteen inches so far," said Mr. Walter.

"Whoa," said Jack again.

"Can we go outside in it?" asked Henry.

"Not until it dies down a little," replied Mrs. Walter. "This is a real blizzard."

"Just like in the movies," said Jack, awestruck.

"Just like in real life," said Olivia.

"But movies are more exciting."

"You don't think real life is exciting?" Olivia opened the dark refrigerator and removed a carton of milk.

"I was just *saying*," said Jack.

Olivia slammed the milk onto the kitchen table. "And I was just *saying*, too. Jeez."

"Olivia?" her mother called from the dining room. "Could I see you for a minute, please?"

"Ha-ha. Now you're in trouble," sang Jack.

"Because of you."

"Olivia, for heaven's sake!" Mrs. Walter set aside the paper, rose from the table, and led her daughter into the living room. "Would you please tell me what's going on?"

Olivia crossed her arms. "All I said was that the storm was like in real life, too. After all, here it is, snowing right in front of us." Olivia waved one arm in the direction of the windows to illustrate her point.

"Jack was just making an analogy," replied her mother. (Olivia said nothing.) "And you picked a fight with him."

"I did not!"

"Would you like me to repeat the conversation I just heard?"

Olivia was tempted to ask if her mother was a recording device, but thought better of it.

"Not only did I hear a foul tone of voice," Mrs. Walter continued, "which, by the way, was completely unnecessary, but I saw you slam the milk carton on the table. Why?"

"Why did I slam the carton down?"

"Why any of it? Why did you pick a fight? You've only been up for five minutes and already you're fighting with your brother."

"Well, he was fighting with me, too."

"Actually, he was defending himself." Mrs. Walter took Olivia's hands in hers. "Something is going on, Olivia, and we need to talk about it. I want you to spill the beans. You haven't been yourself for quite some time."

"Do we have to talk this very second?"

"No, because you'll be a lot less crabby after you've eaten. So please return to the kitchen and eat a civilized breakfast with your brothers. When you've finished, we will go to your room and talk."

Olivia let out a sigh so loud that her father called from the next room, "I hope you didn't roll your eyes just now, Olivia."

Olivia had been about to but stopped in time. She

returned to the kitchen, where she ate bread with peanut butter and drank orange juice while her brothers chattered about building a snow fort with Cole and Travis and Mathias. She left the table when Henry said, "You know what would be funny? If snow forts were called snow farts."

"Okay. I'm ready for my punishment," Olivia announced to her mother.

"Could you please put the sarcasm on hold?" asked her father.

Her mother said only, "Upstairs."

In her bedroom, Olivia, who was wearing a nightgown, a sweater, and her sneakers, sat backward on her desk chair, resting her chin on the top rung. Her mother sat on the edge of the bed, hands clasped, and waited.

"Am I supposed to start?" asked Olivia.

"Please."

"You're the one who wanted to talk."

"Olivia, I have had enough of this. Please tell me right now what is going on. I'm serious."

And with that, Olivia burst into tears. "I don't know! I don't know what's going on!"

"You don't know, or you don't know how to explain it?"

"Explain it, I guess." Olivia wiped her eyes on the sleeve of her sweater.

"Does this have anything to do with Jacob?"

"Yes," said Olivia so softly that she could barely hear the word herself. Her mother waited. At last Olivia said, "Something's wrong with me."

"Tell me what you mean."

"I want to like Jacob, but I just don't. I mean, I do like him! He's one of my best friends. But I don't think I like him the way Melody and Tanya do. You know, I don't *like* like him."

"What's the matter with that, though?"

"The matter is that Jacob *like* likes me. He says I'm his girlfriend. But I don't want him to be my boyfriend, just my friend who's a boy. And," Olivia rushed on, "everyone *thinks* I'm his girlfriend, and that that's very cool. Flora and Nikki, even Ashley."

"And you want to talk to Jacob about this, but you don't know how to do that. Is that right? You don't know what to say to him?"

"That's only part of the problem," admitted Olivia.

"What's the rest?"

"That something's wrong with me. And that's the reason I don't *like* like Jacob."

"Olivia, I really don't know what you mean."

"Well, why *don't* I want a boyfriend? Why does having a boyfriend feel all wrong?"

"Maybe because Jacob isn't the right boy for you. Just because he's your good friend doesn't mean he would be your dream boyfriend. Or maybe it feels wrong because you aren't old enough to have a boyfriend or to be a girlfriend. Don't forget that you're the young-est kid in your school. You're nearly two years younger than most of the students in your grade, and that includes Melody, Tanya, Flora, and Nikki. And Jacob." Olivia nodded miserably. "Honey, do Flora and Nikki want boyfriends?"

"Actually, no. They sort of can't believe Jacob asked me to be his girlfriend. I don't think they're interested in boys yet."

"Doesn't that tell you something?"

"Yes."

"So," said Mrs. Walter, "do you agree that nothing is wrong with you?"

Olivia managed a weak smile. "Yeah."

"Good. But you know you have to talk to Jacob, don't you? You have to tell him what's going on."

Olivia nodded. "I do know. I just don't know what to say. And I can't do it right away. I really can't!"

"Then don't. Wait a few days and think about it. Enjoy the storm in the meantime. But promise me you'll talk to Jacob sometime this week. It's only fair to both of you."

"I promise."

"Good. Now why don't you call Flora and Ruby and see what they're up to? It's going to be an interest-ing day. With the power out, everything in town is closed. The roads are closed, too."

"You don't have to go to work?"

"No. This is a grown-up's version of a snow day."

So Olivia did call her friends — just before the phone service went out. Ruby had answered and was saying, "It's like we're pioneers!" when the line suddenly went dead.

Olivia stared at the receiver in her hand and then announced to her family, "The phones are out, too!"

"Cool!" exclaimed Jack and Henry at the same time.

"Can I go next door?" asked Olivia, eyeing the crystals of snow that were flinging themselves at the windows. "I promise I won't go any farther than Flora's, and when I get there we'll stay inside."

"This," said Jack, "is when we could use a secret passage to connect our houses. It sure would come in handy today."

Olivia recalled the story that all Row House children learned about a secret passage connecting the attics of the homes. When she was younger, she had spent hours searching for it — so had Jack and Henry and later Flora and Ruby — but it was not to be found.

"You can go," said Mr. Walter. "I'll help you."

Olivia bundled into her warmest clothes — boots, hat, mittens, scarf, parka — for the fourteen-yard walk to Flora's house, while her father wrestled with the storm door and attempted to shovel some of the snow from the stoop.

"You'd better take this with you," he said, handing her the shovel when at last they were standing on the bottom step. "You're going to have to clear off Min's stoop in order to get inside."

Olivia could barely hear her father over the howling wind. "This really is exciting!" she said, her mood already improving.

She set out across the yard, wading through blowing snow that reached well above her knees. She saw that against the Row Houses the snow had drifted as high as her head.

"Are you okay?" her father shouted from the Walters' doorway.

Olivia turned and managed to give him the thumbs-up sign, but she had to close her eyes against the snow, which pricked at her face like needles. When she reached the front of Flora and Ruby's house, she couldn't see the stoop, but she stumbled to the door, rang the bell, and started shoveling.

"Olivia!" exclaimed Flora as the front door opened. She peered at her friend through the storm door. "I can't believe you're here. Let me help you."

Five minutes later, Olivia, her wet clothes drying in the kitchen, sat in Flora's bedroom with King Comma in her lap.

"See? We really are like pioneers, aren't we?" said Ruby, who was curled on the bed.

"Pioneers with nonworking telephones and computers and refrigerators," said Flora.

"Well, you know what I mean. Isn't this fun?"

"Yeah, it is," agreed Flora.

"I wonder what the pioneers would do during a blizzard," said Ruby.

"Oh, you know. Make soap and brooms and stuff," replied Olivia. "I think they'd keep working. Catch up on all their indoor chores."

"*We're* not going to do chores," said Flora. "I think we should make hot chocolate —"

"How?" asked Olivia. "No microwave, no stove."

"Oh, yeah. I guess we are a little like pioneers."

"Do you think Min would let us boil water in the fireplace?" asked Ruby.

"Absolutely not. She'd have a fit. I know. Let's go downstairs and set up the card table in front of the fireplace, where it's warm, and play board games. With Min. She would like that."

And that was how Olivia spent the morning. At lunchtime, she and Flora and Ruby and Min ate jam sandwiches and apples and noticed that the snow was letting up. In the middle of the afternoon, the power came back on, and by dinnertime, the people on Aiken Avenue were starting to shovel their walks and driveways.

"We won't be back to normal for a couple of days, though," said Min.

"Maybe school will be closed on Monday after all," said Ruby hopefully.

Olivia didn't care whether school was open or closed. She felt better than she had in weeks and went home to apologize to her family.

CHAPTER 14

A Family for Mary

It was amazing, Mary Woolsey thought, how quickly Camden Falls could clean up after a blizzard. She remembered a snowstorm, one not quite as severe as the recent one, that had closed the town for a week when she was a child. But that was before the days of hulking snowplows with salt spreaders that could do their jobs in almost any conditions. She looked through the front window at her yard, which was buried under more snow than she had seen in a long time, and at her walk, which had been shoveled on Sunday, and at the street, where streaks of pavement glistened under a clear blue sky. Only four days since the storm and already the roads were open and life in Camden Falls had returned to normal. Even school had opened on Monday with only a two-hour delay.

Now it was Wednesday and Mary was preparing for the event she had had to postpone from Sunday. Her little family, the one that consisted of herself and her two cats, was about to expand considerably. Her relatives were coming.

Mary clasped her hands, took one more look out the window to be sure her guests would be able to park somewhere on the street, and returned to her kitchen. What did one serve to people who would be arriving at eleven o'clock in the morning? Lunch? Brunch? Snacks? Mary was making coffee and had baked cookies and coffee cake and had bought Danishes at Sincerely Yours. She was prepared to fix sandwiches, too, and she had sliced fruit and made a yogurt dip to go with it.

"We have plenty of food," she said aloud to Daphne and Delilah, her elderly orange cats. "That's not the problem. The problem is where to sit. We won't all be able to fit around the kitchen table. I guess we'll just have to eat on our laps in the living room. Goodness, I've never had so many guests."

Mary returned to the window and clasped her hands again. She checked her watch. "Ten fifty-four," she announced to the cats. "I wonder if they're the kind of people who will be on time." She left the window, eased onto the couch, and drew Delilah into her lap. "Goodness me, what have I gotten myself into? What are we going to say to one another? These people are my relatives, but I don't know them at all. What if conversation runs out — or worse, what if they're all horrible? They could be rude and loud and . . . and I've invited them into my home." She stroked Delilah's back. "Of course, I did speak to Catherine over the phone, and she sounded very nice." (Catherine was Mary's half sister.)

Daphne, who was curled tightly next to Mary, suddenly sat up and pricked her ears forward.

"What is it?" asked Mary. "Was that a car door? And here I thought you were deaf." She patted Daphne, set Delilah gently on the floor, and once more crossed the room to the window.

A van had pulled up in front of her tiny house, and climbing out of it were seven adults, one of them cradling an infant to her chest.

"Oh, my," said Mary, and she opened her door.

"Mary Woolsey, is that you?" A woman who was somewhat younger than Mary halted on the path through the gardens.

"Yes," said Mary hesitantly.

"Oh, good. We've got the right house then. I'm Catherine Landry, your sister." Catherine continued her approach, but she slowed down and regarded Mary uncertainly.

Mary had wondered how she was supposed to handle such a situation, and she'd even glanced through a book on manners that her mother had bought years ago, but she hadn't been able to find a single mention of how to greet a sister that you were meeting for the first time when you were seventy-eight. She had finally decided that a handshake might be the thing. Best not to appear overly demonstrative with someone you didn't know. But as Mary stepped outside and saw more clearly the woman who was approaching her — with an armful of flowers, Mary now noticed, and a face that might be her very own — she stopped and put her hand to her heart. And Catherine dropped the flowers and folded Mary into her arms.

Mary felt tears running down her wrinkled cheeks and knew that Catherine was crying, too.

"To think, after all these years," said Catherine. She drew back from Mary but held tight to her hands as she turned to the people who had crowded behind her on the walk. "Mary, this is my husband, Gil, this is our daughter, Missy, and these are our sons, Marc and Richie. Over there is my niece Cassandra — she's my youngest brother's daughter — and that's Lizette, Marc's wife. I suppose you can guess who's in Lizette's arms."

Mary smiled. "Your new granddaughter." She let go of Catherine's hands and stepped forward to greet the rest of her guests, just as Catherine said, "Would you like to hold her?" and reached for the baby.

Missy was looking at the flowers on the ground and laughing. "Mother!" she exclaimed. "What a mess! I think we're overwhelming Mary. Anyway, it's freezing out here and Mary isn't wearing a coat. Let's go inside first."

"Of course," said Catherine. "What was I thinking?"

Missy stooped to gather the flowers, and Mary led

her guests indoors. When their coats had been hung in the closet, and Daphne and Delilah patted and fussed over, and the coffee poured and pastries served, Mary sat in the living room and looked at her company.

She put her hand to her heart again. "I scarcely know where to begin," she said, and laughed nervously. "A whole lifetime to catch up on and I don't know what to say."

Catherine smiled and reached into a bag that Gil had carried inside. "Maybe this is the way to start." She handed Mary a photo album and opened the worn cover. "My mother kept this," said Catherine. "The very first picture in here is of me not long after I was born." She turned a page. "And here I am with my father — our father, I mean." She looked at Mary. "I don't want to make you uncomfortable. I have no idea how you felt when you learned that your father had started another family after leaving you and your mother. But since you went looking for us, I assume you want to know about your relatives."

"Oh, I do!" said Mary. "I have no idea why our father did the things he did, and the truth is that what he did hurts, but you're family, and I absolutely want to get to know you."

Catherine squeezed Mary's hand. Then she turned back to the album and said, "We lived in Wisconsin when I was born. That was our house. I was the first of four children, by the way, so you can see that you have a lot more family to meet. When I was two, we moved to Vermont, but we returned to Wisconsin a couple of years later and that's where my brothers and I grew up."

"How did you find your way to Massachusetts?" asked Mary.

"I went to college in Worcester and just stayed on. My brothers are still in Wisconsin, though."

"Then *my* brothers and I went to the same college in Massachusetts that Aunt Catherine had attended," spoke up Cassandra, "and we stayed here, too."

"I could have wound up anywhere in the world," said Catherine. "Anywhere at all. And I settled forty miles from a sister I didn't know I had. But that I'd always wanted," she added. "Did I mention that before? I'd always wanted a sister, and then it turned out I actually had one."

"And I longed for a family, and look what I got," said Mary.

"A whole passel of relatives, and you're stuck with us!" said Richie.

Catherine and Mary turned pages in the photo album while Cassandra and Richie fixed plates of fruit and sandwiches and carried them into the living room. Daphne and Delilah settled themselves in Marc's lap. The baby slept placidly in Lizette's arms.

Mary looked at one photo after another of her father. Her father grinning at the camera; her father with one shirtsleeve rolled up, showing off his muscles;

her father pushing baby Catherine on a swing. At last she said, "And my father never . . . mentioned me?"

"He didn't," replied Catherine. "I'm sorry."

"Don't be sorry. I'm just trying to put the pieces together."

"You said he sent you money after he left you and your mother?"

"Regularly, until he died," said Mary. "Although, of course, I didn't realize that the reason the money stopped coming was *because* he had died. I didn't even know who was sending the money. My mother knew, but she didn't tell me. And she allowed me to believe that he had died in the fire at the factory where he worked."

"A lot of family secrets," commented Richie.

"I didn't know that Dad had had another wife until after his death," said Catherine. "Then I was curious to find out if I had half brothers and sisters, but I had almost no information to go on. And then I received your letter." She smiled at Mary. "Thank you for searching."

Mary looked around at her guests and said, "Perhaps you could tell me about yourselves."

"You mean, who are we people?" said Gil with a laugh. "I'll start. I met Catherine not long after she had graduated from college. I'd grown up in Rhode Island, but Catherine and I settled here, and I started my own business, a packaging company."

"I'm going to law school," said Cassandra.

"I'm a writer," said Marc.

The conversation continued, the daylight began to fade, and when Mary looked at the clock, she was astonished to see that the afternoon was nearly over.

"We have something for you," said Catherine as everyone stood and stretched and began to put on their coats. She reached into the bag once more and handed Mary an album with a fabric cover and the words *Mary's Family* spelled out in brass letters.

"I tried to find a photo of each of your relatives — all the nieces and nephews and in-laws, everyone. They're all in here."

"She labeled them so you can keep us straight," said Gil.

"Thank you," whispered Mary.

"Remember," called Missy as she climbed into the van a few minutes later, "we're going to get together at Easter, okay? You aren't rid of us."

"We'll get together at all the holidays," added Catherine.

As the van drove off, Mary closed the door to her little house and said to Daphne and Delilah, "That was the best gift my father could have given me."

CHAPTER 15

A Job for Flora

"Hi, Aunt Allie! I'm here!" Flora poked her head around her aunt's front door. She had hurried there as soon after school as possible, which wasn't terribly soon since, thanks to the storm, she could no longer ride her bicycle around town and instead had to pick her way along slushy sidewalks.

Allie hurried into the hallway from her study. "Flora? I didn't know you were coming today," she said in a hushed voice. "Janie's asleep."

"Sorry." Flora lowered her voice. "I hope I didn't wake her."

Allie ducked back into her study and listened to the baby monitor for a few moments. "All quiet," she announced.

"How long has she been sleeping?"

"About fifteen minutes."

"Oh." Flora couldn't hide her disappointment. "So she just went down for her nap."

"Sorry, honey, she seems to be on yet another schedule. The last few afternoons she's been falling asleep between three and three-thirty — and not waking up until nearly five."

"Oh," said Flora again. "Well . . . what would you like me to do? I'm here to help. Hey, maybe she'll just take a short nap this afternoon!"

"I hope not," said Allie. "She'll be awfully fussy tonight if she doesn't get enough sleep now."

Flora looked around the house, which appeared quite tidy. "Do you want me to start the laundry or something?"

"You know, I'm really in pretty good shape. Thanks to you," Allie added quickly. "I'm caught up with the housework and I'm meeting my deadlines."

"So . . ." Flora was now searching desperately for a job that might need doing, preferably one that would keep her occupied until whenever Janie awoke. She had planned to wheel her cousin casually by Mr. Barnes's house a few times that afternoon, hoping he might come outside to chat. At which point Flora would have made sure to bring up Aunt Allie.

"Honey," said Allie, "let's go sit in the living room. We need to have a talk."

"Did I do something wrong?" asked Flora, and she could feel her face begin to flush.

"Oh, no! Of course not." Allie led her niece to the couch and patted the cushion next to her. "Flora, you have been the biggest help I could have imagined. Truly.

I don't know what I would have done without you these last few weeks. But the truth is, I'm feeling more confident now, and since you helped me get so organized, I'm not behind with my work. I feel I can manage things much better than I could in the beginning."

"So you don't need me anymore?" said Flora in a very small voice.

"No, that isn't it at all! I just think I need you less often and at different times. However," (Allie paused) "I don't want your talents to be wasted."

"My talents?"

"You are one of the most giving, generous, and helpful young women I know."

"Thank you."

"But I think maybe other people need you now more than I do. I heard that Three Oaks is looking for volunteers, and I was wondering if you might consider working there, maybe once a week. You could come by here on the weekends, at times when Janie's awake. What do you think?" When Flora didn't say anything, Allie continued, "I know how much you want to spend time with Janie, and believe me, Flora, we're all going to spend plenty of time together, you and Ruby and Min and Janie and I. When you're just a little older and Janie is just a little bigger, I hope you'll be able to baby-sit for your cousin while I go out. But right now, while she's *so* little and I'm staying at home most of the time, well, as I said, I think other people need you more than I do."

"I do like Three Oaks," said Flora, examining a button on her shirt and recalling the many visits she'd paid to the Willets. "But what do you think I could do if I volunteered there?"

"You've already helped teach a sewing class," Allie reminded her. "And they must need volunteers to do a hundred different things: run errands, read to people, maybe help teach other classes, make holiday decorations, even work in the mail room. I don't know for sure, but you could find out easily enough."

"How would I get all the way out there, though? It's too far for me to ride my bike."

"I'm sure something could be arranged. Someone will be able to drive you. Three Oaks has shuttle service, too."

"Yeah," said Flora.

"And then on the weekends you can visit Janie."

"When she's awake."

"When she's awake," agreed Aunt Allie.

Flora turned and looked mournfully across the street at Mr. Barnes's house, but her aunt had a point. There really wasn't any sense in Flora's hanging around every afternoon, waiting for Janie's naps to end. She stood and reached for her coat. "Okay. I think I'll go home and call Nikki. Maybe her mom knows about volunteering at Three Oaks. Or maybe I'll call Mr. Willet. I'll be able to talk to him right away."

"Excellent," said Allie.

Flora made her way slowly back to Aiken Avenue,

her mind on Three Oaks. She recalled that once or twice when she'd visited the Willets she'd seen people walking through the halls wearing blue smocks, each with a large yellow handprint on the front and the words *Helping Hand* on the back. Maybe Flora could become a Helping Hand. She'd seen Helping Hands in the Three Oaks library and gift shop, behind the reception desk, and pushing wheelchair-bound residents to appointments or meetings. Allie was right. There were probably a hundred things Flora could do to help out.

By the time Flora reached the Row Houses, her heart was lighter. She opened her front door with a flourish and called, "Ruby?"

"Upstairs!" Ruby replied. "Writing my composition!"

"What composition?"

"'My Imaginary Pet,'" Ruby called back. "I'm inventing a little tiny fur-covered human called a Babbler."

Flora sprawled on the couch in the living room and dialed Nikki's number. When no one answered, she called Mr. Willet.

"Well, if this isn't a treat," said Mr. Willet. "How are you, Flora?"

"I'm fine. How are you? How's Mrs. Willet?"

"I'm fit as a fiddle, thank you, and Mrs. Willet's holding her own. What can I do for you?"

"I was thinking," said Flora, "about volunteering at Three Oaks. Is there anything for kids to do there?"

"Hmm. Well . . . I have seen kids volunteering here from time to time."

"As Helping Hands?"

"Yes, I think so."

"I'd be happy to do anything. Teaching the class with Min was fun, but I could run errands or visit people."

"You know," said Mr. Willet, "there are a lot of group activities here for people like Mrs. Willet who have Alzheimer's. Music programs and art projects and even cooking projects. The group leaders might need volunteers. Why don't I make a couple of phone calls and see what I can find out about the Helping Hands?"

"That would be great," Flora replied. "I'd really appreciate it.

Two days later, Saturday, the phone rang just as Flora was getting ready to walk to Aunt Allie's with Ruby.

"Don't answer it!" cried Ruby. "Janie's awake. Come *on*!"

But Flora looked at the caller ID and said, "No, wait. It's Mr. Willet. I want to talk to him. Hello? Mr. Willet?"

"Hi, Flora. I have good news for you. I spoke with a very nice woman here last evening named Mrs. Jasper. She's the volunteer coordinator, and she said she'd be happy to meet you and that she can always use another Helping Hand."

"Yes!" cried Flora.

"She'll be in her office on Monday. You can call her then. I'll give you her phone number."

Flora wrote the number down, feeling very professional, and when she hung up the phone, she turned to Ruby and said seriously, "I have a job. I mean, a real job, with a boss."

"Really? You do? What is it?" asked Ruby, who politely refrained from saying that personally she preferred to be her own boss.

"Well, I don't actually have it yet," Flora admitted. "I'm supposed to call this volunteer coordinator on Monday. But I'm pretty sure I'm going to become a Helping Hand at Three Oaks."

"Cool. What are you going to do?"

"I don't know."

"Who's going to drive you to Three Oaks?"

"I haven't figured that out yet. But I will. And I'm going to arrange everything by myself."

On Monday, Flora hurried home from school, running a good part of the way, and the moment she'd put her things in her room and caught her breath, she found the piece of paper on which she'd written Mrs. Jasper's phone number and dialed it. She realized her hands were shaking.

"Eleanor Jasper," said a warm voice, and Flora relaxed because she could tell, just by the sound of those two words, that Eleanor Jasper was the sort of person who could make things right, repair frayed nerves, and solve any problem.

"Hi, Mrs. Jasper," said Flora, and she had to pause to stop her voice from squeaking with excitement. "My name is Flora Northrop. I think Mr. Willet talked to you about me?"

"Oh, yes! Hello, Flora. I'm so glad you called."

Flora and Mrs. Jasper spoke for several minutes, and by the end of the conversation they had agreed that Flora should come to Three Oaks for a trial day of work the following week.

"Thank you very much, Mrs. Jasper," said Flora, remembering various things Min had told her about applying for jobs — manners (good ones, obviously), using people's names in conversation. She hung up the phone, dialed Mr. Pennington, and told him her news. Then she said, "I just have one problem, and Min said I could ask you about it. Is there any chance you could drive me to Three Oaks next week? I know it's a lot to ask."

"I'd be happy to do that," Mr. Pennington replied. "I'll visit with the Willets and take you home when you're finished."

"Thank you very much, Mr. Pennington," said Flora soberly, as if she were applying for a job with him, too. But after she had clicked off the phone, she scooped up King Comma and twirled him around the room in celebration.

CHAPTER 16

Caught!

Ruby was pleased. Her self-improvement plan seemed to be working. Many very nice things had taken place as a result of Ruby's stick-to-itiveness (a favorite phrase of Min's). And Min seemed to be quite taken with the change in her granddaughter.

"Ruby, I'm mighty proud of you," she had said several times in the past couple of weeks. (The third time she'd said it, Ruby had noticed a slight frown cross Flora's face.)

"Thank you," Ruby had said modestly.

"Your teacher has only called once so far this semester, and that was to tell me that not only have you been handing in all your homework on time, but you got an A on your geography quiz."

"Give me a blank map of the U.S. and I can tell you where every state goes," Ruby had told her proudly.

"That's fabulous, honey. You certainly are growing up."

Not long after this conversation, the phone had rung and Flora had announced to Min that Ms. Angelo was on the line.

Ruby's eyes had widened. In the past, calls from Ms. Angelo had not brought good news. The worst call had been the one on the day after Thanksgiving when Ms. Angelo had informed Min that she'd decided to put Ruby on probation.

"What did you do now?" Flora had asked Ruby as she'd passed the phone to Min.

"Nothing! I swear!" Ruby had exclaimed, frantically trying to figure out whether this was actually true.

But when Min had hung up the phone, she'd been smiling. "Congratulations, Ruby," she'd said. "Ms. Angelo just told me that you've been doing beautifully recently, and that if your hard work continues, she'll take you off probation."

"Really? *Off* probation?" Ruby had cried.

"Off probation. Truly, honey, I can't . . . I can't get over the change in you."

(Ruby suspected that Min had been about to say that she couldn't *believe* the change in her, but that was okay. Ruby couldn't blame her, all things considered.)

So . . . Ruby tallied up the good things that had happened lately. Her teacher had noticed the improvement in her schoolwork and had called Min. Min had praised Ruby. Ms. Angelo had also noticed Ruby's improvement and had called Min. Min had praised

Ruby again. Best of all, in Ruby's estimation, was one thing that *hadn't* happened: Min had not noticed that the owl was missing. And (speaking of the owl) Ruby had located a replacement and was socking away her hard-earned dollars as the Doer of Unpleasant Jobs in order to be able to purchase it as soon as possible.

Now it was late on a Saturday morning and Ruby, her weekend homework already started, was off to do several chores for her clients. The first stop was at Mr. Pennington's house, where she was to shovel his walk and his front stoop. Since the blizzard, snow had fallen regularly in Camden Falls, and Ruby and her friends had even had a snow day at last. The most recent snow — four more inches — had fallen the night before, and Ruby wanted to tackle Mr. Pennington's walk before lunchtime.

She arrived at his house with her own snow shovel (well, one of Min's) and announced, "Here I am!"

"Wonderful, Ruby," said Mr. Pennington. "Just in time. I need to go into town."

"I'll be done in a jiffy."

Ruby huffed and puffed and chopped ice and piled snow. When the cleared walk gleamed behind her, she ran back to Mr. Pennington's stoop, collected her pay, and continued to the Fongs', whose walk she had also agreed to shovel. She stuffed several more bills in her pocket as she left the Fongs' house later and, as she walked to her third job, tried to calculate how much money she'd earned altogether, and how much she still needed before she could walk back into the snooty man's jewelry store and show him that she had enough to buy the crystal owl. She envisioned herself dumping a bag of change and dollar bills onto his pristine counter, quarters rolling in every direction, and made a mental note to have the money converted into larger bills before it came time to make her purchase.

Whistling, Ruby made her way through the neighborhood to the home of Min's friend, Mrs. Angrim.

"I'm so glad you're here, Ruby," said Mrs. Angrim when she opened the door. "You don't know how long I've been putting off this project." She led Ruby into her kitchen. Every single cabinet door was open, and every item from every cabinet was piled on the table and the counters. Mrs. Angrim handed Ruby a roll of shelf paper. "Are you sure you're ready for this? It's a hideous job."

It was hideous, but lining the shelves with paper, each piece of which had to be cut to fit its space, would also take a long time, which meant that Ruby would earn a lot of money, and that was fine with her.

"I'm ready," said Ruby. And she set to work.

Several hours later, when the job, which in fact *had* been rather hideous, was at last finished, Ruby was grubby, tired, and most of all, hungry. But she felt very pleased with herself when Mrs. Angrim looked at her neat-as-a-pin kitchen and her cheerful polka-dotted shelves and said, "Ruby, this is wonderful. Thank you!" And she paid Ruby handsomely for the job well done.

Ruby walked back to the Row Houses, whistling a tune that she thought was from one of Min's Gershwin CD's and might be called "Walking the Dog." Images of grilled cheese sandwiches and chocolate cake floated through her brain.

"Flora?" she called as she opened the front door. She fingered the bills in her pocket as she ran up the stairs.

She stopped when she reached her bedroom.

The vacuum cleaner was in the middle of the floor and Flora was kneeling next to it, sifting through the contents of the bag, which she had dumped onto a sheet of newspaper. She looked as if she might have been crying.

"What's going on?" asked Ruby. She tried to ignore her rumbling stomach.

"I —" Flora started to say, and Ruby noticed that her sister's hands were shaking. "I guess I broke something of yours," said Flora miserably.

"You guess?" Ruby's eyes drifted to her china animals, but she didn't notice that any were missing. "What do you mean, you guess?"

Flora sat down with a thump. "I was vacuuming in here. That's my job this weekend — vacuuming the bedrooms — and I was right over there by your bureau, and suddenly I heard something go up the hose.

Something like, well, china. It clinked. Only I swear I hadn't knocked anything off your bureau. I *swear*."

Ruby looked once again at the rows of animals, all of which seemed to be accounted for, and a horrible idea began to take shape in her head. She cast her mind back to the day when she'd brought the crystal owl into her room, and she envisioned its tragic fall to the floor, saw herself with the broom and the dustpan, frantically sweeping up the shards. She must have missed a piece of glass in her haste. And now Flora had slurped it up with the vacuum.

"I've been going through the stuff in the vacuum cleaner bag," said Flora, getting to her knees again, "and I did find that piece of glass." She pointed to a slender chunk, as pointy and as sharp as a dagger, which she'd set apart from the pile of dust and lint in the middle of the newspaper. "It's the only thing that could have clinked. But what's it from? Did I break something of yours? If I did, I'll pay you for it. I'm really sorry," she said.

Ruby let out her breath. Okay, now what? The easiest thing, she said to herself, was to lie. Just tell her sister that she didn't know what that piece of glass could be from and that nothing in her room seemed to have been broken. Or . . . she could let Flora think she actually had broken something of Ruby's (but what?) and pay her for it. Ruby could then put the money toward the owl.

But when the new, improved Ruby Northrop

opened her mouth, she was very surprised at what came out of it.

"You didn't break anything," she said. "I did."

"What?"

"I broke something of Min's."

Flora's eyes narrowed. "You broke something of Min's? Here in your room?"

"Yeah." Ruby drew herself up as straight as possible. "And I'm going to tell you the truth about what happened." She felt that honesty should be part of the self-improvement plan.

"Well . . . good," said Flora uncertainly.

"I was looking through Min's drawers," Ruby began.

"You were *what*?"

"Looking through her drawers. You know, just to see if she had anything interesting —"

"Ruby! You can't do that! It's an invasion of privacy!"

"Well, I did do it, and anyway, tell me you've never snooped. That's all it was. Snooping."

"Giving it a cute name like *snooping* doesn't make it any better," said Flora.

"Well, all right, so I found this box of stuff that had belonged to Mom and one of the things in the box was an owl and I just wanted to introduce it to my animals," said Ruby desperately, seeing the look on her sister's face. "So I brought it in here and I dropped it and it broke and I decided to improve myself and I found another owl at the new jewelry store and I'm saving enough money to buy it and when I do I'll put it back in the box and Min will never know the first one got broken." She attempted a smile. "And they all lived happily ever after!"

Flora was gaping at Ruby. "What you did is wrong for *so* many reasons," she said finally. "Snooping, lying —"

"I haven't told any lies!" Not yet, anyway, Ruby thought.

"Yes, you have. By not telling the truth. That's like a sin of omission."

"I don't know what you're talking about."

"I'm talking about telling Min what you did."

"No way!"

"Ruby, you absolutely cannot let Min think that the new owl — if you even manage to get away with all this — was Mom's. The real value of the one you broke wasn't how much it cost. It was the fact that it belonged to Mom. You can't fool Min like this. It is completely unfair."

"If I tell her what happened, it will upset her. Is it fair to upset her?"

"None of this is fair. The owl must mean a lot to Min or she wouldn't have kept it. And now it's broken, and buying her a new one is not going to make things right."

"But if she never knows what I did — Flora, I'm very close to getting away with this."

"Listen to yourself! You just said 'getting away'! You know what you're doing is wrong!"

"It's none of your business, so stay out of it."

Flora glared at her sister. "All right. For now. I'll stay out of it for now. But this isn't over, Ruby."

"Yes, it is."

"No, it absolutely is not."

Flora finished cleaning up the mess in Ruby's room and left without saying another word.

CHAPTER 17

Just Friends

"Olivia?"

Olivia, who had been attempting to jerk open her temperamental locker door, jumped at the sound of the voice that had spoken directly into her ear. She dropped a stack of books and a pair of sneakers as kids streamed around her, eager to begin their afternoon activities.

"Jacob!" she said, gasping. "You startled me!" What she wanted to say was, "What were your lips doing so close to my earlobe?"

"Sorry. I'm sorry," replied Jacob, who did indeed look sorry. "I didn't mean to scare you." He helped her gather her things. "Where do you want them?"

"I was about to sort them out. Half of the books stay here, the others come home with me." Olivia jammed the sneakers onto a shelf.

Jacob stood woodenly by the locker while Olivia

then selected four books and placed them in her backpack.

"Olivia?" he said again.

"Yeah?"

"What's wrong?"

Olivia turned to him. "What do you mean?"

"I mean, I know something is wrong. I think it has to do with us, but I'm not sure. Whatever it is, we need to talk about it."

Olivia sighed, feeling unbearably guilty. On the day of the snowstorm, which now seemed rather distant, she had promised her mother she would talk to Jacob that week. And she'd meant to talk to him. She really had. Instead, they'd spoken less and less, and seen each other less and less outside of school. Olivia had thought about the conversation, and what she would say to Jacob, and how he might respond, and the more she'd thought, the more uncertain she'd become. About everything. Well, about everything except the fact that she knew she didn't want to be Jacob's girlfriend.

What on earth should she say to him now? How could she tell him any of her thoughts without hurting his feelings? She could barely explain her feelings to herself. Furthermore, and this was something Olivia knew she could mention to no one — not her mother, not Flora, not Nikki, and certainly not Jacob — one small, conceited piece of her wasn't ready to give up her enviable status as Jacob's girlfriend. The image of Tanya or Melody swooping down on an Olivia-free Jacob was absolutely horrifying. What would she do if one of them became Jacob's next girlfriend?

And yet, here stood Jacob, waiting for Olivia to answer him. She knew it was time to talk.

Olivia set her backpack on the floor and straightened up. "You're right. We do need to talk."

"Oh, boy," said Jacob.

"I know. I'm sorry."

"So what's going on?"

Olivia almost laughed. "Jacob, we can't talk here!" Jacob stared at her. "I mean, let's go —" Where *could* they talk? Certainly not at Olivia's house, where her brothers would undoubtedly engage in some creative eavesdropping. Definitely not here in school. "Want to go get a slice of pizza?" Olivia asked at last.

"Sure." Jacob had the look of someone who was on his way to a torture chamber.

Olivia and Jacob walked along Main Street, Olivia waving at shopkeepers and at Jackie and Donna in the post office, and then stopping in Sincerely Yours to tell her father where she and Jacob were going to be for the next hour. At College Pizza they slid into the booth against the back wall. And stared at each other.

"So?" said Jacob. He transferred his gaze to the slice of pizza in front of him, cheese drooping off the edges of the paper plate. His hands remained folded in his lap.

"Well, okay." Olivia had absolutely no idea where to start and finally decided that maybe she was thinking about things too much. "Okay," she said again. "The thing is . . ."

"The thing is, you're breaking up with me, right?"

Olivia's eyes jumped to Jacob's, startled. "Um, yes. But," she continued hastily, "not because I don't like you."

"You're breaking up with me because you like me?"

Olivia could see a smile on his lips, and she smiled back. "You know what I mean. Yes, I like you. I *really* like you. You're one of my best friends. But being your girlfriend . . . doesn't feel right."

"I had a feeling that's what was wrong."

"I'm sorry. I didn't know how to tell you. Especially since I *do* like you so much. That makes it harder. I don't want to hurt your feelings and I hope we can always be friends."

"But just friends." Jacob took a sip of his soda. Olivia attempted a bite of pizza. "Why?" asked Jacob after a few moments.

"Why what?"

"Why does being my girlfriend feel wrong?"

Olivia shrugged. "I don't know. Maybe it's not so much that it feels wrong as that it doesn't feel right."

"That doesn't help."

"This is the part I don't understand myself. It's like when two people have the opposite reaction to the same thing. How do you explain it? They both see the same story on the news and one person says, 'Oh, how interesting!' and the other person says, 'That's horrible! How could something like that happen?' You know?"

"I guess."

"Jacob, I don't know if now is the right time to ask this question, but *do* you think we can stay friends? It's so —" Olivia tried to control her voice, which she realized was wobbling dangerously, "so important to me. If you weren't my friend, I don't know what I'd do." She fumbled for her napkin and dabbed at her eyes. Any moment now, her nose would start to run.

"Of course I want to be your friend," Jacob replied. "I guess I was just hoping I could be more than your friend, too. But if I have to settle for just friends, well . . . I can't imagine *not* being your friend."

Olivia managed a smile. "That's how I feel. At least we agree on that. So, we can still do our homework together? And sit together at book club meetings?"

"And eat lunch together?" asked Jacob.

"Yes. But maybe every now and then Flora and Nikki and I will sit by ourselves. We haven't seen much of each other lately."

Jacob nodded. He glanced down at his half-eaten slice of pizza and then across the table at Olivia's nearly untouched slice. Olivia thought he was going to ask if he could have her piece. Instead he said, "Do you want to go?"

It took Olivia a moment to realize that Jacob,

whom Nikki thought of as a human Dustbuster, had lost his appetite and was willing to leave behind a good quantity of uneaten food.

"Yeah." Olivia slid out of the booth and struggled into her parka and scarf and hat and gloves while Jacob, who was wearing only a jacket, watched her. The prospect of walking home alone and worrying about how long it would take for Melody or Tanya to get wind of what had happened left Olivia feeling helpless. So she was pleased when Jacob said, "Want to go for a walk?"

"Sure!"

Weighed down by their backpacks and their thoughts, Olivia and Jacob walked slowly along Main Street.

"This is nice," said Jacob eventually.

"What is?"

"This. Just walking along together."

"We can still do it. Whenever we want."

"Yup."

Olivia felt something loosen in her chest. "Want me to call you tonight?"

"About Mr. Barnes's assignment? Definitely."

Olivia flashed him a genuine smile as she turned and left for Aiken Avenue.

"Flora?"

"Hi, Olivia."

"What are you doing?"

"Right now? My homework. Why?"

"I just wondered." Olivia lay on her bed, her feet propped on the wall, her head hanging over the side. She was halfway through her own homework and in ten minutes would call Jacob. Before that, she wanted to talk to Flora. "Are you in the middle of something? Can you take a break?"

"I can talk. What's the matter?"

"Well . . . I broke up with Jacob this afternoon."

Olivia wasn't sure what kind of reaction she had expected from Flora — maybe a shriek or a gasp or an exclamation of "Oh, that's awful! Are you all right?" Instead, after a little pause, Flora said, "I kind of thought that might happen. I mean, not necessarily today, but soon."

"You're kidding! You did?"

"Yeah. I knew you weren't happy and I figured it had something to do with Jacob. I'm really sorry, Olivia. But I guess this is what you want, right?"

"I think so. Flora? Why didn't you say anything to me?"

"About Jacob? I don't know. We haven't seen each other much lately, and anyway, I didn't want to seem nosy. I figured you'd let me know if you wanted to talk."

"I wasn't purposely *not* talking to you. It's just that everything was so mixed up, I didn't know what to say. I didn't talk to anyone about it. Well, except Mom, but that was because she forced me."

"It's okay."

"One of the reasons — one of the many reasons — we broke up was because I felt like I didn't get to spend enough time with you and Nikki anymore."

"Really?"

"Really."

"I missed you, Olivia!"

"I missed you, too."

"So you feel better about everything?"

"Definitely. Well, except for one thing."

"Which is?"

"That I won't know what to do if Jacob decides to go out with Tanya or Melody now."

"With Tanya or Melody?! Are you out of your mind?"

"I —"

"Olivia, do you really think Jacob wants to spend time with either one of them? He can't stand them."

"Oh. Yeah. You're right."

"You should have talked to me sooner."

Olivia laughed.

And when she went to bed that night, she felt very grateful for her friends. For Flora, for Nikki, for Ruby and Willow. And for Jacob.

CHAPTER 18

Bad-bye

"He's here," Nikki whispered to Tobias.

Her brother got up from his chair in the living room and peered through the front window. Driving slowly along the lane to the Shermans' house was a truck with a U-Haul van attached to it. "All right," said Tobias under his breath.

In an hour or so, thought Nikki, her father would be gone, traveling back to South Carolina with his boxes and his clothes, the pieces of his life that had cluttered Nikki's house for months and made her feel attached to a presence that she wanted gone.

"Is it Daddy?" asked Mae, who was sitting before the dollhouse. She jumped to her feet.

Nikki knew her sister was wondering if perhaps one more gift would be forthcoming — not because Mae was greedy, but because Mr. Sherman's last few visits had become, one by one, quieter and shorter and angrier, and Mae's enthusiasm about her father had turned to uncertainty.

"Yes. He's here," Nikki said. "And you know what's going to happen today, don't you, Mae?" Behind her, Nikki heard her mother open the front door.

"It's time for Daddy to leave?"

"Yes. And he's going to take his things with him, all the things he's been packing up. We probably won't see him for a long time. Remember, Mommy talked to you about that."

"I know." Mae frowned. She looked at her mother posed hesitantly at the partly open front door and at Tobias standing behind her with his arms folded severely and then at Nikki, who was gripping Mae's hand a bit too tightly. "Why is everyone so mad?" she asked. She pulled her hand away, adding, "Ow, you're hurting me."

"Sorry," said Nikki, and at that moment Mr. Sherman stepped into the house.

After a brief silence, Mae said in a small voice, "Hi, Daddy."

Mr. Sherman glanced at the overstuffed boxes and garbage bags piled by the door. "I see you got everything ready for me."

"Nothing to do but load up the van," said Tobias. "Just trying to be helpful. We thought you'd like to get on your way early."

Mr. Sherman snorted. "Very thoughtful."

Nikki felt a pain take hold in her stomach. The arrangements had been finalized, hadn't they? Divorce, custody, everything was in place and couldn't be changed, could it? She put her hand over the blossoming pain. She knew she would feel better if she could be sure that when the van turned onto the county road she would never have to see her father again, unless it was her decision. But now was not the time to ask her mother about this.

Tobias hefted a box and started outside.

"Not wasting a minute, are you?" asked Mr. Sherman.

Tobias ignored him.

"Do you want to come inside and see the dollhouse?" Mae asked her father. "I made little teeny tiny books for the family to read."

"That's great, Mae. But I think your mother and brother are pretty eager to see the back end of me."

Mae laughed. "The back end!" But when she realized no one else was laughing, she said, "What does that mean?"

"It means they can't wait to get rid of me. Come on, Mae. See if you can lift any of these boxes. Help hurry me on my way."

"I don't want to hurry you. . . ." Mae's voice trailed off. She looked at the boxes, then at her father. "What do you really want me to do?"

Tobias returned to the house and, grunting, lifted

another carton. "Am I the only one who's going to load the van?" he said over his shoulder as he struggled down the porch steps.

"Daddy?" Mae asked.

"I really couldn't care less what you do, Mae." Mr. Sherman grabbed the nearest garbage bag, this one filled with clothes he hadn't been able to fit into his suitcases.

Nikki reached for Mae, but Mae slapped her sister's hand away and ran upstairs.

"Let her go," said Mrs. Sherman. "Let's just get this over with."

Nikki, Tobias, and their parents worked wordlessly until all the boxes and bags had been loaded into the van.

"Good," said Tobias grimly.

Mr. Sherman started for the house again.

"Where are you going?" asked Nikki's mother.

"There are a few more things in there that are mine."

For several terrifying moments, Nikki thought that one of those things might be Mae. When her father returned from the house carrying the table that had sat in front of the couch, Nikki sagged with relief.

"Hey!" exclaimed Tobias. "What are you doing?"

Mr. Sherman hoisted the table into the van and then turned to stare at Tobias. "What does it look like?" He began to speak loudly and slowly. "I . . .

AM . . . PUTTING . . . THIS . . . *TABLE* . . . IN . . . THE . . . *TRUCK.*" He shoved several boxes aside to clear space.

"You can't take the furniture!" exclaimed Tobias.

His father waved his hand toward the table, like a game show host presenting a prize. "I think I just did."

"That isn't part of the agreement," Mrs. Sherman spoke up. "The furniture stays here."

"The furniture I bought and paid for?" Mr. Sherman walked heavily into the house again, this time emerging with a throw rug. "Nikki? Make yourself useful and get the lamp out of your mother's bedroom. And the chair by the front door."

"This is not part of the agreement," said Mrs. Sherman again. "You're violating the agreement."

"I have a right to these things and a lot more, agreement or not."

Nikki watched her brother take a step closer to her father. She watched her mother take a step backward, toward the house and Mae. She felt the pain in her stomach increase a notch, as if someone had turned a wrench.

"Tobias," called Mrs. Sherman. "Forget it. Let him have the things."

Nikki realized that there wasn't room for much more in the van anyway.

"No!" said Tobias. "He's not getting away with this." He climbed into the van and began tossing things onto the driveway.

In an instant, in one beat of a hummingbird's wing, Mr. Sherman leaped into the van and shoved Tobias out. Tobias landed on the table, which splintered under his weight.

"Howie, no!" cried Mrs. Sherman.

"You stay out of this."

"No! Not this time." Nikki's mother advanced on the van.

"I'm going to call the police!" Nikki suddenly shouted.

Everyone ignored her. Nikki saw Paw-Paw peek out from behind one of the sheds and prayed he would stay out of sight.

"I am! I'm going to call them right now!" Nikki had intended to start for the house, but her feet seemed rooted to the snowy ground.

Tobias was standing shakily now, brushing at his pants, and Nikki tried to determine whether he was hurt. Mr. Sherman tossed the throw rug back into the van, pushed past Tobias, then past Nikki and once more hurried through the front door. This time he returned carrying Mae's dollhouse, the furniture and dolls rattling from side to side, Mae's carefully arranged rooms in disarray.

Mae was behind him. "Daddy!" she cried, stepping onto the porch in her bare feet. "What are you doing?"

"You're going to come visit me sometime, aren't you, Mae? I want you to have something to play with when you do."

Mae's face crumpled. "I thought that was mine to keep."

"'I thought that was mine to keep,'" repeated Mr. Sherman. "Boo-hoo-hoo. Well, we all have our disappointments. You'll want your doll, too, when you come to South Carolina. Go get that for me, Mae."

"No."

"All right. You leave me no choice." Mr. Sherman set the dollhouse down and again disappeared through the front door. When he stumped back out of the house, he was carrying Peppy by one stiff arm. Mae let out a howl. "That's mine! That's *mine!*"

"Well, you can visit her in South Carolina."

Tobias picked up the dollhouse.

"You take one step toward the porch with that," said Mr. Sherman, "and —"

Tobias glared at his father and then took one giant step in the direction of the porch.

Mr. Sherman dropped Peppy and grabbed Tobias by the shoulders. Tobias lost his balance and fell but held tight to the dollhouse.

Mae screamed and her mother gathered her in her arms.

Nikki felt panic overtake her. "Okay! Now I really am going to call the police!" She fled for the house and returned with the cordless phone. She held it up so her father could see it. "Nine," said Nikki, "one —"

"Hang up the phone and I'll let go of Tobias."

Nikki clicked off the phone.

"Go," Mrs. Sherman said to Nikki's father in an even voice that Nikki knew meant trouble. "Take the dollhouse and the doll, put them in the van, and leave. You've made your point."

Mae, who had buried her head against her mother, pulled away and looked up at her. "Why are you letting him take them?" she wailed.

"Honey, not now," whispered Mrs. Sherman. She turned toward Mr. Sherman again. "GO!" she screamed so loudly that Mae burst into fresh tears and fled to Nikki. "GO!"

"Mom," said Tobias. "Calm down."

"I want Peppy," Mae sobbed.

"We'll get you a new doll," Nikki told her, although she knew that wasn't the point.

Mr. Sherman stood defiantly in the back of the van, unmoving. Nikki held up the phone again and began to punch in numbers. "Nine, one, ONE!" she shouted.

Mr. Sherman closed the van and climbed into the truck.

Nikki slipped the phone into her pocket.

Mr. Sherman started the engine, rolled the window down, and leaned out. "Don't you have a kiss for me, Mae?"

Mae's face turned a frightening shade of red. "Bad-bye! Bad-bye! I hate you! I will never visit you. Bad-bye!"

Mr. Sherman roared off.

Nikki sank to the ground, legs shaking. Mae slumped into her lap. A moment later, her mother was sitting on one side of her, and Tobias on the other.

"It's over," whispered Mrs. Sherman.

Nikki watched the back of the van to be sure.

CHAPTER 19

Flora Northrop, Working Girl

Flora, belted into the front seat of Mr. Pennington's car, watched the February countryside glide leisurely by. If Mr. Pennington had been a faster driver, the countryside would have flown by, but he was not fast. He was cautious, glancing frequently into his mirrors, watching the sides of the road for errant squirrels and bunnies, and grumbling when cars approached too quickly from the rear.

"It's almost Valentine's Day," said Flora, feeling she should make conversation. "I can't believe it."

"I'll bet Three Oaks will be all decorated."

"Really?" said Flora, having a hard time imagining adults celebrating Valentine's Day.

"Sure. Very festive. Three Oaks gets decorated for everything."

Flora didn't answer.

"Nervous?" asked Mr. Pennington.

"A little." In fact, Flora was quite nervous. She was

on her way to the interview with Mrs. Jasper, which would be followed by a trial hour of work.

"Ever been on a job interview before?"

Flora slid her eyes over to Mr. Pennington, who was intent on the road. He tooted the horn at a squirrel. Was he teasing her? Flora decided he wasn't.

"No," she replied. "But Min has told Ruby and me lots of things about being a responsible employee and about how to behave on an interview. She told us that once somebody came into Needle and Thread about a sales position and the first thing she said to Min and Gigi was that she didn't like to sew. Next she said she would prefer not to have to talk to the customers."

Mr. Pennington laughed. "I suppose she didn't get the job."

"Not only that, but Min told her she needed to improve her attitude." This was something Flora had heard her tell Ruby, although not lately.

"Would you like to have a pretend interview now?" asked Mr. Pennington, swerving to avoid what turned out to be an oak leaf. "I could take Mrs. Jasper's role and ask you questions."

Immediately, Flora felt her face flush. The very thought of role-playing made her want to jump out of the car. Role-playing was far too much like acting, and acting was Ruby's world. "That's okay. Thank you. I think I know what to do. I'm supposed to be polite. And at the end, if Mrs. Jasper says, 'Now, is there anything

you would like to ask *me*?' I'm definitely supposed to
ask something. It will make me sound eager. So the
question I prepared is, 'Would you ever like me to
teach another sewing class or help teach one?' Then, if
Mrs. Jasper doesn't know about the class Min and I
taught, I'll tell her about that."

"Perfect," said Mr. Pennington. "I'm sure you'll
do fine."

Flora felt that the interview would indeed be fine,
but she was still nervous. Ten minutes later, as she sat
across from Mrs. Jasper at her desk, she could feel her
heart thumping. She clasped and unclasped her hands
and realized they were sweating.

"So you're the famous Flora Northrop," was the first
thing Mrs. Jasper said. She smiled warmly, and Flora
smiled back at the wide face and the dark brown eyes.

"The famous Flora?" she repeated.

"I've heard all about you from Mr. Willet. And I
spoke to several of the residents here who took a sewing class with you and your grandmother."

Flora relaxed. "That was really fun," she said. "I
enjoyed meeting everyone."

"I understand you visit Three Oaks often?"

"Pretty often." Flora hesitated. She didn't want
Mrs. Jasper to think she was bragging, but she added,
"I know my way around fairly well, and I've spent
time with Mrs. Willet in the wing for people with
Alzheimer's."

"Do you feel comfortable there? Are you comfortable with people who might say strange things or make funny noises?"

Flora nodded. "Yes. I mean, I wish they didn't have Alzheimer's, but their behavior doesn't bother me."

Mrs. Jasper rewarded her with another smile. "And why do you want to work here?"

Flora chose her words carefully. "The very first time I came to Three Oaks," she said slowly, "I have to admit that I thought it was depressing. But that was because when I saw Mr. Willet's apartment it was still completely empty, and I hadn't known that Mrs. Willet was going to live in a place where the door was locked all the time. But then Min — that's my grandmother — and my sister and I started visiting here, and I saw that Mr. Willet was happy, and I saw how much everyone cared for Mrs. Willet. I saw how busy Mr. Willet was, too. He joined committees and he's always taking trips and classes and going to lectures and movies. He told me he's going to start tutoring kids at a school that's near here.

"Every time I visit Three Oaks, I discover some other wonderful thing — the gift shop, the art gallery, the crafts room. I decided I wanted to be part of a place that's made Mr. Willet so happy. He's really lucky to be able to live here. So is Mrs. Willet. Anyway, I'll do whatever you ask me to do. I mean, if I can start working here."

Mrs. Jasper got to her feet then, and Flora looked up at her in horror. The interview was over, that much she could tell. What had she done wrong?

But Mrs. Jasper's face broke into a smile again. "Flora, I like your attitude. Are you ready for a test run as a Helping Hand?" She reached into a box behind her and pulled out a blue smock with a yellow handprint on the front. She handed it across the desk to Flora.

"Really? I can be a Helping Hand?"

"Well, like I said, this is a test run. But I have a feeling you'll be back here regularly. By the way, will you be able to come one afternoon a week?"

"I think so. I'll have to talk to Mr. Pennington about that. He's a friend of Mr. Willet's and he brought me here today. Min works full-time, so she can't drive me. But I know I can figure something out. Mr. Pennington likes to visit the Willets."

"Let me know if you run into difficulty. We'll see what we can do about transportation. For now, why don't you put the smock on, and I'll introduce you to Dee. She's working at the front desk, and I'm sure she'll have things for you to do."

Flora was kept very busy for the next hour. Wearing her Helping Hand smock, she delivered flowers to two apartments, escorted a visitor to the coffee shop, helped a resident carry groceries from her car to her kitchen, and assisted at a music program in Mrs. Willet's wing.

"Hi, Mrs. Willet!" said Flora brightly when she spotted her old neighbor seated in a semicircle of wheelchairs.

The wheelchairs had been arranged in front of a piano, and waiting patiently at the piano was a young man wearing a straw hat and a shirt with bold red and white stripes. He was smiling cheerfully. A card had been placed on top of the piano. It read RAGTIME JOE.

"This looks like fun," said Flora to Mrs. Willet.

Mrs. Willet's attention had been drawn to a spot on the carpet. "Bum-bum-bum-bum," she murmured.

Flora looked around and saw that absolutely nobody was paying attention to Ragtime Joe. In fact, a number of the residents were asleep, and one, whose head was tipped back, was snoring loudly.

Ragtime Joe appeared unconcerned by his audience.

A nurse wheeled another man to the entrance to the activities room and signaled to Flora, who made room for him in the circle.

"I think that's everybody," said Joe, and he settled himself at the piano and began to play a jaunty tune. Two of the sleeping residents woke up, and Mrs. Willet raised one hand and said loudly, "Shoes!" Or maybe, "Choose!" Flora couldn't tell which, but Mrs. Willet looked content. When Ragtime Joe said, "Clap your hands!" she clapped them smartly two times before her fingers found the bottom button on her sweater and her attention drifted again.

Twenty minutes later, the door to the activities room opened quietly and a man wearing a Helping Hand smock entered. He leaned down to Flora and whispered, "Mrs. Jasper wants to see you in her office. I'll take over here for you, okay?"

Flora nodded. She checked her watch and was surprised to find that more than an hour had passed. She hurried back to the office.

"How's our newest Helping Hand?" Mrs. Jasper asked her.

Flora grinned. "Does that mean I have the job?"

"You have the job."

"Oh, thank you! When do I start?"

"Next week, if you can. Why don't you and Mr. Pennington and I discuss transportation?"

On the way back to Camden Falls that afternoon, Flora said, "I can't believe I have a real job! Well, a volunteer job, but that's a real job, isn't it?"

"It certainly is," Mr. Pennington replied. "Min is going to be very proud of you."

"*I'm* proud of me. I was *so* nervous when I was talking to Mrs. Jasper, but I think the interview went well. I can't wait to go back next week. Thank you for driving me. I really appreciate it."

"It's my pleasure. Shall we go to Needle and Thread and tell Min the good news?"

"Definitely," Flora said, and added, "just think, I am now Flora Northrop, Working Girl."

CHAPTER 20

Ruby's Reward

Ruby sat on the floor of her bedroom, counting her Valentines. "Twenty-seven," she said aloud. "That's a nice haul."

From her own bedroom, Flora called, "How many did you send?"

There was a slight pause. "Thirty-four."

"Huh."

"Well, twenty-seven is still a lot. How many did you get?"

"I didn't bother to count."

"I'll bet you didn't need to count. You could just look at them spread out in front of you and say, 'Oh, I got four.'"

Flora didn't respond.

"You know what my best Valentine's Day present was?" Ruby called.

"Your *best* one? How many did you get?" It was

February 15th, and the previous day had not included the giving of any gifts that Flora was aware of.

"Well, just one. Ms. Angelo called a few minutes before you got home this afternoon and said my probation will be over on March first if I keep up my good work. That's in just two weeks!"

"Yippee," muttered Flora.

Min's reaction to the news was slightly different. When she returned from Needle and Thread that evening and heard about the phone call, she said, "Ruby, the change in you has been remarkable. You really are growing up. It's been weeks since I've had to remind you to do your chores."

"You haven't had to remind me, either," Flora pointed out as she finished setting the table in the kitchen.

"You never need reminding," Min replied.

"You're practically perfect in every way," added Ruby. "Just like Mary Poppins. I, on the other hand, am not. I mean, I'm not naturally perfect. I have to work at it. You're so lucky. Things come easily for you."

"In any case, Ruby," Min continued, "I'm very pleased with everything — your chores, your homework, the news about your probation."

"We get progress reports in school tomorrow," said Ruby. "I hope mine will show the results of all my efforts."

"Luckily, you're modest," said Flora.

"Luckily, you're jealous," said Ruby.

"Girls," said Min. "Please."

Ruby's progress report was better than even she could have imagined. "I might almost make straight A's on my next report card!" she exclaimed at dinnertime as Min read her teacher's comments. "Flora, have you ever made straight A's?"

"Twice."

"When was the last time?"

"Ruby, I don't know. Sixth grade, okay?"

"J-E-A-L-O-U-S," sang Ruby. "Min, would you like more pasta?"

Min was shaking her head in disbelief. "Ruby, I'm mighty proud of you, honey. You've worked very hard. I think we ought to celebrate. We'll go out to dinner this weekend, the three of us and Rudy Pennington. How would you like to go to Fig Tree?"

"Really? We can go to Fig Tree?" squeaked Ruby.

"You're kidding? We're going to Fig Tree?" squeaked Flora.

Fig Tree was the most expensive restaurant in Camden Falls, and a reservation was made there for special occasions only.

Min glanced briefly at Flora and then said, "Yes. Fig Tree it is. Good work, Ruby."

Ruby finished her supper with a smile on her

face. "May I be excused?" she asked, and when Min said yes, Ruby carried her plate to the sink, rinsed it off, and stashed it in the dishwasher. "I have to do my math homework," she announced, and disappeared upstairs.

Ruby sat at her desk with two worksheets before her. Twice she picked up her pencil and then put it down again. Her hand drifted to the bottom drawer of her desk. She glanced into the hallway. Empty. She listened for the sound of footsteps on the stairs. Nothing.

Silently, Ruby opened the drawer and found the envelope she'd stuffed into the back. It wasn't labeled, since she didn't want anyone to know what was in it — and it was very fat, since it was stuffed with bills. Ruby slid them out and counted them. She now had enough money so that she could go back to the fancy jewelry store and tell the haughty clerk that he could put the crystal owl on hold for her. She would be able to pay for it in just a few weeks. Pay for it *in full*. She had worked hard, and very soon she would be able to right her wrong.

"What's that?"

Ruby jumped at the sound of the voice, and the bills scattered across her desk. She scrambled to gather them into a pile. "Haven't you ever heard of knocking?" she exclaimed as she slid them back in the envelope.

"Your door was open," Flora replied.

Ruby knew she'd been careless. What if Min had seen her? "Well, you still could have knocked."

Flora ignored her. She sat on Ruby's bed. "I suppose that's the owl money?"

"Yup." Ruby returned the envelope to the desk and shut the drawer firmly.

"So you're really going through with this?"

Ruby scowled at her sister. "How many times do we have to talk about it? Min's not going to be able to —" She glanced at her open door, crossed the room, closed it, and sat at her desk again. "Min's not going to be able to tell the owls apart," she said quietly. "She'll never know anything happened, so she won't have to get upset. I'm just trying to spare her feelings."

"Spare yourself, you mean."

"Well, what do you want me to do?"

"Tell Min the truth!"

"I haven't lied to her! And if I do tell the truth . . ." Ruby paused and injected an impressive quaver into her voice. "If I t-tell her," (sob) "it w-will just m-make her start reliving the a-accident and everything again."

Flora shook her head. "Do you really believe what you're saying?"

"Look, if you think what I'm doing is so wrong, why don't *you* tell Min about the owl?"

"Because then I'd be a tattletale."

"Yup."

"And anyway, *you* should be the one to tell her."

"Exactly. This is none of your business. You even said so yourself."

"That's not the point and you know it. You did something wrong, and you know the correct way to fix the problem. But you're taking the easy way out."

"The *easy* way out?! You think what I've been doing is easy?"

"I guess lying and fooling people *is* pretty hard." Flora stood up. "I hope you enjoy your special dinner, Ruby. It's exactly what a liar and a cheater deserves."

The dinner at Fig Tree took place on Saturday evening.

"Fancy dress," Min announced when she returned from Needle and Thread that afternoon. "A chance to get all gussied up."

"Um, do we actually have to wear dresses?" asked Ruby.

When Min said yes, Ruby didn't press the point.

Min, Flora, and Ruby in their best dresses, and Mr. Pennington in his best winter suit, arrived at Fig Tree at six-thirty and were shown to a round table near the fireplace.

"Isn't this festive?" said Min.

"And cozy," added Mr. Pennington. "There's nothing cozier than a fire."

"Dinner is on me," announced Min, "and this is a celebration, so please order whatever you want."

"Could I have a cocktail?" asked Ruby.

"You may have a Shirley Temple," Min replied, peering at Ruby over her reading glasses. "You too, Flora."

"I'll just have a seltzer, thank you," said Flora.

The waiter took their drink orders and Ruby studied her menu. "Prime rib!" she exclaimed.

Flora kicked her under the table, then leaned over and whispered, "That's the most expensive thing on the menu."

"Well, I never almost got straight A's before. And anyway, Min said to order what we want."

When the drinks arrived, Ruby reached for her Shirley Temple, but before she could take a sip, Min held her glass aloft and said, "Just a moment. I would like to make a toast. To Ruby, for all her hard work and for demonstrating what a responsible and mature young lady she's becoming."

Ruby looked across the table at her grandmother's beaming face and saw that her eyes were glistening with tears. She detected a quaver (a genuine one) in her voice.

"Um, thank you," said Ruby.

"I know these last two years haven't been easy for either of you," Min continued, "and I'm proud of both my girls. You've overcome a lot of obstacles. And Ruby, you've made some remarkable choices in the last few weeks. Good for you."

Ruby took a swallow of her Shirley Temple then, but an uncomfortable feeling was creeping into her chest. Remarkable choices. *Had* her choices been remarkable? (She knew what Flora would say: remarkably bad.) *Had* she been responsible and mature? Ruby had thought so. The decision to replace the owl in secret had been made in order to spare Min's feelings.

Hadn't it?

The waiter returned to the table. "Are you ready to order?" he asked.

Min gestured to Ruby. "You go first. The dinner is in your honor."

"I'll have the chicken," said Ruby in a small voice.

"You were pretty quiet at dinner tonight," Flora said later as she perched on the edge of Ruby's bed. "I think Min wondered what was wrong."

Ruby said nothing. She couldn't forget Min's face as she'd made the toast.

"You're starting to feel guilty, aren't you?"

"No!"

Flora looked smug. "Yes, you are. And you should be."

"I am not. Anyway, the new owl is already on hold for me. I went to the store yesterday. I told that mean guy that I want to buy the owl as a birthday present for my grandmother, and he agreed to hold it for me for a month."

"So you told another lie!" cried Flora.

"I told *a* lie. And I haven't lied to Min."

"Not telling her about the owl is like lying."

"*Like* lying. *Like* lying. It isn't *actually* lying."

"Girls? What's going on in there?" called Min from the hallway.

"Nothing," Flora said, and flounced back to her room.

Ruby threw herself onto her bed and buried her head underneath the pillow.

CHAPTER 21

Just Sew

"Everybody ready?" called Nikki's mother from the front door of the Shermans' house.

"Ready!" replied Nikki.

"Mae?" said Mrs. Sherman.

"Almost ready." Mae struggled down the stairs, carrying a bulging backpack.

"What on earth is in there?" asked Nikki.

"Some books, a sandwich, a banana, my crayons —"

"Mae! Why are you bringing all that to Needle and Thread?"

"You said we were going to spend the day there. So I brought lunch and also some stuff to do in case I get bored."

"But, Mae, we're going to be working on the quilt. And you're going to be a helper. There will be plenty to do. Plus, I think Min and Gigi will have food for us."

Mae set her backpack down and eyed it longingly.

"I made a bologna and peanut butter sandwich. My favorite. Can I at least bring that?"

Nikki wrinkled her nose. "If you must."

Mae fished the sandwich out of the backpack and followed her mother and Nikki to the car. She strapped herself into the backseat, and as Mrs. Sherman turned the car around she said, "Did we see the back end of your husband?"

"What?" asked Mrs. Sherman.

"That day, before he took my doll, your old husband said you wanted to see the back end of him. *Did* we see his back end?"

"I'm pretty sure we did," replied Mrs. Sherman. "Remember? We talked about that? I have custody of you, and you don't have to visit your father unless you want to."

"Okay," said Mae.

In the days since Mr. Sherman had left, Nikki's family had tried to resume their lives. Tobias had gone back to school and had worked out some arrangement for making up his missed classes and exams. Nikki had gleefully turned her father's cleared-out workshop into a shelter for the stray dogs. And Mrs. Sherman was setting aside a little money each week to replace Peppy and the dollhouse.

Nikki looked out the window as her mother sped along the county road. The trees were still bare, but the snow that had continued to fall throughout February had melted. She cracked her window open and felt a warm breeze on her face, smelled spring in the air.

"Tell me again what we're doing today," said Mae from the backseat.

"Flora had an idea," Nikki told her. "You know the community center? Where you might take ballet lessons this summer?"

"Yeah."

"Well, they need some extra money."

"I could use some extra money," said Mae.

Nikki smiled. "The community center needs a *lot* of extra money, though, or they might not be able to stay open. So Flora had the idea that if everyone helped make a quilt, Min and Gigi could auction if off at Needle and Thread and give the money to the community center to help them out."

"We're going to make a quilt today?" said Mae. "I don't know how to make a quilt."

"You don't have to know how. Everyone who stops by the store is just going to decorate squares for the quilt. Then Min and Gigi and Flora will sew the squares together. You might want to start thinking about your own quilt square, Mae. The theme is Camden Falls. You could make a picture of something you like in town — your school or the library. You could draw it on your square, or I could show you how to embroider it, if you want to use thread instead of markers."

Mae was quiet.

"Mae?" said Nikki.

"*Shh.* I'm thinking."

"I'll pick you up after work today," said Mrs. Sherman as she dropped Nikki and Mae off in front of Needle and Thread. "Have fun!"

Needle and Thread was already busy.

"Look how many people are here," said Nikki as she opened the door for Mae.

Seated around a large worktable in the back of the store were Mr. Pennington, Robby Edwards, Olivia, Ruby, two girls from Ruby's class at school, and a woman Nikki didn't recognize.

"Hi!" called Flora, hurrying to greet Nikki. "This is great! We have three finished squares already, and they look wonderful. Do you want to help or make your squares first?"

"I'll help," Nikki offered.

"I want to make a square," said Mae, "since I've been thinking about it and I have a really great idea."

Nikki settled Mae at the worktable, and the morning sped by. She helped Flora, who was handing out squares of muslin and demonstrating various needle-work techniques.

"You can draw with fabric paints," Nikki told each new arrival. "You can use actual quilting techniques — piecing and appliqué — or you can embroider a picture. You can even embellish your picture with ribbons and buttons, almost like scrapbooking. Just remember that each square has to have something to do with Camden Falls. That's our theme."

Nikki watched the finished squares pile up. Robby had used fabric paints to draw a picture of the Row Houses. "I couldn't get them all on one square, though," he said. "I had to use three. They go next to each other like this, okay?" He arranged the squares in a row.

Flora's square, with neatly appliquéd figures, showed a scene on Main Street.

Ruby, whose talents lay in areas other than crafts and sewing, handed Flora a square with a painting of a witch on it, complete with a pointed hat and a broom.

"Um, Ruby?" said Flora. "The theme is Camden Falls."

"Hello, I starred in a play called *The Witches of Camden Falls*," replied Ruby. "That was about our town's history."

"Do you think," said Flora, trying to choose her words carefully, "that you might want to include that somewhere? Here, I can show you how to embroider the title of the play along the bottom. It's easy. Really."

Mae's square, when she finally finished it, having worked huddled on the floor in a corner of the store so that no one would steal her idea, was a list of book titles, which she had written out in her best handwriting in red, blue, and green fabric markers. She handed the square to Nikki.

"Huh," said her sister, sneaking a glance at Flora, "*The Wind in the Willows, A Bear Called Paddington, James and the Giant Peach, The Invention of Hugo Cabret* . . . Mae, this —"

"Isn't it creative?" said Mae proudly. "You said to make something about Camden Falls, and that's a list of my favorite books at the library."

"Oh," replied Nikki. "I see. That's great, Mae." She paused. "You know what might make it even better? If you added something — just some little something — to let people know how much the library means to you."

"Okay," Mae said, and returned to her corner.

At one o'clock, Gigi called from the counter, "Lunch break! Our treat! Everyone stop working!"

And as if by magic, a stack of pizzas appeared from College Pizza; soda and water were delivered, cold, from the market; and Olivia's father arrived with a tray of chocolates and pastries from Sincerely Yours.

"Perhaps not the most nutritious lunch," said Gigi as Min cleared the worktable and set out the food, "but it's fun."

"And delicious!" said Mae, whose mouth was full of bologna and peanut butter.

When the food had been eaten, Nikki, Flora, Olivia, and Ruby assembled the sewing supplies again, and the afternoon was spent once more helping with the creation of quilt squares. Nikki saw images of the ice cream shop, the movie theatre, the Christmas tree in the town square, the community center, Mayor Howie, and scenes (non-witch) from Camden Falls history, the annual Halloween parade, and, of course, Needle and Thread.

"We have too many squares for one quilt," Flora announced later in the afternoon. "Either that, or we'll have to make the world's largest quilt."

"Could you make two quilts?" asked Nikki.

"Hey, that's a good idea," said Flora. "It would be a lot of work, but then we could auction off both of them and raise even more money. I'll talk to Min and Gigi."

At the end of the long and satisfying day, Min told the last few customers that thanks to their hard work and the work of everyone who had dropped by the store, they would indeed be able to make two quilts. "We expect to finish them by the beginning of the summer," she added. "We'll hold the auction here at Needle and Thread. Spread the word. And be generous with your bids."

"Min!" exclaimed Flora in a hushed voice. "That's not exactly tactful."

"Oh, for heaven's sake," said Min. "It's for a good cause." She raised her voice. "Be *very* generous."

Nikki smiled and realized that she had not thought of her father in hours.

CHAPTER 22

The Sad Farewell

The March day that Mr. Pennington had chosen for Jacques's farewell was sunny and much warmer than usual for early spring.

"Jacques would have liked today," Flora remarked to Min over breakfast. "This was his favorite kind of weather. He probably would have spent the morning lying on the bench in Mr. Pennington's backyard."

"When he was a puppy, he would have spent it flying around the yard, chasing butterflies and leaves," Min said.

"I wish I had known Jacques when he was a puppy. I only knew him when he was an old dog."

"We'll all have a chance to talk about Jacques today and to share our memories of him. That's what Mr. Pennington wants."

"Do you think it will make him sad?" wondered Flora.

"Probably. But in a good way. It's always nice to remember the ones we've loved."

Flora slid her eyes toward Ruby, who suddenly needed to pay a lot of attention to the milk she was pouring on her cereal.

"Yes," agreed Flora. "It's nice to remember the ones we've loved. And the things we loved about them. And the things that were important to them."

Ruby's face grew pink, but still she said nothing.

"Yup, it sure makes us feel comforted to have memories and, oh, *mementos* of people we loved, people we miss now. Being able to hold on to things —"

Ruby shoved her chair back from the table, stood up so fast that she nearly tipped her chair over, and marched out of the kitchen.

"You didn't finish your breakfast!" Flora called after her.

"Is there anything going on that I need to know about?" asked Min.

Flora pondered this. Technically, yes, there was. But it wasn't Flora's place to tell Min. Not yet, anyway. Not if she could convince Ruby to change her mind.

"No," said Flora, but she couldn't meet her grandmother's eyes because she knew Min didn't believe her.

At eleven o'clock that morning, the Row House neighbors, as well as Nikki and Mr. Willet and several other people who had known and loved Jacques, gathered in Mr. Pennington's backyard. Standing in the warm sunshine on any other unexpectedly lovely day, Flora would have felt contentment and a sense of promise wash over her. But on this morning, as she looked at Mr. Pennington, who was holding a tin box and whose lips were trembling, she felt close to tears herself. She reached for Min's hand, and Min squeezed it.

"Thank you," Mr. Pennington began. "Thank you all for coming."

"You're welcome," said Robby loudly.

Mr. Pennington smiled at him. "Jacques had a lot of friends," he went on, "and if he could see all of you gathered together in his yard it would make him very happy. Jacques loved company. In fact, he loved a lot of things. He was an enthusiastic dog.

"I was thinking that today we might take turns remembering Jacques. When we're finished, we're going to spread his ashes in our backyards — all of the yards — since Jacques considered them his own. And considered all of you his family."

"Excuse me!" Alyssa Morris, Lacey's little sister, raised her hand. "Is this like *The Tenth Good Thing About Barney?*"

Flora, who had been about to burst embarrassingly into tears, now tried to stifle a laugh. But Mr. Pennington, who had once been a schoolteacher, answered Alyssa's question patiently. "Ah. You're thinking about the book about the boy whose cat dies. Well, I suppose this is like that, except that we don't have to limit ourselves to ten things about Jacques. We can each say as much as we like, all right?"

Alyssa nodded seriously. Then she asked, "Can I start?"

"Absolutely."

"Okay. Well," (Alyssa clasped her hands together) "I used to be afraid of dogs when I was little, but Jacques helped me get over that. He was nice and friendly and he never bit."

Olivia's brother Henry raised his hand, and Mr. Pennington called on him. "Jacques liked to play fetch with me," said Henry. "I'll miss that."

Mr. Willet spoke up (without raising his hand). "When Mary Lou was first showing signs of Alzheimer's, she liked to sit with Jacques and talk to him. She could sit with him for half an hour or more. I think Jacques brought her a feeling of peace."

"Jacques was a good companion," said Min. "And a good friend to you, Rudy."

"He really was a friend," agreed Dr. Malone. "I think he understood how people were feeling. He was very sweet with Margaret and Lydia when their mother died."

Over and over, the people gathered in Mr. Pennington's yard recalled that Jacques had been sweet, friendly, loyal, and good company. Then Mr.

Fong said, "Remember the day he stole our chicken? He let himself in our back door somehow and stole a chicken off of our kitchen table."

"Once I made a gingerbread man," remarked Lacey, "and he ate an arm off of it."

Mr. Pennington smiled. "He did manage to get into trouble, too, but most of the naughty things he did made me laugh."

"I once saw him skid around a corner and fall in his water bowl," said Olivia.

"Well," said Mr. Pennington at last, "I think it's time to return Jacques to the earth. Alyssa, let's start in your yard and work our way back to the Fongs'."

Flora, Olivia, and Nikki linked arms and followed the neighbors through the backyards to the Morrises' house.

"I've been thinking," said Nikki as they walked along. "Mr. Pennington should adopt another dog."

"He says he's too old," Flora replied. "He doesn't want to adopt a dog that would outlive him. It wouldn't be fair to the dog."

"But he could adopt an older dog. That would be perfect. It's harder for older dogs to find homes because most people want to adopt puppies."

"Hey, that *is* a good idea," said Olivia. "He could adopt a dog that's five or six."

"Is it too soon to talk to him about it?" wondered Nikki.

"Maybe a little," said Flora. "Let's wait a few weeks. I can ask Min what she thinks."

They reached the Morrises' yard, and Mr. Pennington opened the tin box. He reached inside, withdrew a handful of gray and white ashes, stooped, and spread the ashes around the base of a rosebush. At the Hamiltons' house, the Malones', Flora's, and Olivia's, he spread a bit of his old companion. He skipped his own house, stopped at Robby's, went on to the Fongs', and then returned to his yard.

"The last bit," he said, "will go right here." And he spread the remainder of the ashes under the bench. "Good-bye," he said. "You were a wonderful friend."

"Good-bye," murmured the Row House neighbors.

Flora hugged Mr. Pennington. Then she walked back to her house, arms once again linked with Nikki's and Olivia's. Ruby trailed behind, alone.

CHAPTER 23

Springtime

Here is Camden Falls, Massachusetts, at the end of March, which is unseasonably mild this year. A man seated on a stool in the window of Frank's Beans, the coffee shop, turns to his companion and says, "I could have predicted it. A long, warm autumn and now an early spring."

Jackie, who works in the post office, waits until there's a lull in business, and then, fanning her face with a catalog, says to her only customer, "Not as many snowstorms as usual this year."

At Sincerely Yours, Robby props the door open with a brick to allow fresh air into the store, and Olivia's father says, "I have a feeling it's going to be a hot summer. I hope our air conditioning holds out."

At Three Oaks, Flora, wearing her Helping Hand smock, sits on a terrace with Mrs. Willet and several other residents in wheelchairs.

"Isn't this nice?" says Flora, feeling the sun on her

face. "Can you believe we can sit outside at the end of March?"

No one answers her, but Flora thinks the four old women are enjoying the sunshine and the breeze and the birdsong. They sit in silence until the door to the terrace opens and a nurse signals to Flora.

"Okay," Flora replies. She rises, unlocks the brakes on Mrs. Willet's wheelchair, and pushes her inside to the day room, where the nurse is waiting. One by one she brings the other women inside, too. "I have to go now," she announces, and again no one answers. But when Flora bends down to kiss Mrs. Willet's cheek, her old neighbor says, "Good-bye," and takes her hand.

Flora smiles. "I'll see you next week."

"Yes," says Mrs. Willet.

Flora finds Mr. Pennington waiting for her in the lobby. "Did you have a nice visit with Mr. Willet?" she asks. As they walk to his car she tells him about her afternoon. The ride home is quiet, though, until Flora says, "Mr. Pennington? Excuse me if this is too personal — or nosy — but have you thought about getting another dog?"

"That's neither personal nor nosy," replies Mr. Pennington, braking slightly at the sight of a twig in the road. "I have thought about getting another dog. But I haven't made a decision yet."

Several miles outside of Camden Falls, off the county road, Mae Sherman is playing in her yard with Paw-Paw. She has managed to fit a Red Sox cap on his broad head, and now she calls to her sister, "Nikki, what if Paw-Paw were a professional baseball player?"

Nikki has no idea how to answer that question, but she smiles. Mae looks content; it's been several days since she asked a question about her father.

"Want to help me feed the dogs?" Nikki asks, and Mae jumps to her feet. The stray dogs have been coming to their new shelter every day. Nikki keeps the bowls filled with chow and fresh water, and she's spread blankets on the floor. She's pleased to see that the dogs use the shed in bad weather.

The mild afternoon begins to draw to a close. Peek in the windows of Needle and Thread, and there are Min and Gigi at the back of the store. Two customers are choosing fabric, and while they make their decisions, Min and Gigi bend over the worktable, the pieces of the first of the two Camden Falls quilts spread before them.

"Flora can help us with this over the weekend," remarks Min.

"We ought to be able to finish both quilts by June, don't you think?" says Gigi.

"Probably. Maybe then we can have an auction party here at the store."

Down the street and around two corners are the Row Houses. The younger kids — Alyssa and Travis Morris, Cole Hamilton, and Olivia's brothers — have spent the entire afternoon in their backyards and running in and out of one another's houses. Now their parents call them inside for supper and to start their homework.

At the Hamiltons' house, Cole's father is warming lasagna in the oven. "Come sit down," he says to Cole and Willow, motioning to the kitchen table. "I want to talk to you. Your mother will be coming home in a month, and we need to start thinking about how things will change."

Cole doesn't know whether to feel pleased or frightened.

Several doors away, Olivia carries the phone into her bedroom, gently closes the door, and dials Jacob's number. "Hi," she says when she hears his voice. "Did you start your composition yet?"

In another part of town, Mary Woolsey settles herself in an armchair after a day of work at Needle and Thread. She pulls out her knitting and says to Daphne and Delilah, "I think I'll be able to finish this tonight." It's a sweater for her grandniece, who will be visiting soon, along with Mary's sister.

And in a small house on a street on the east side of town, Mr. Barnes picks up his telephone and notices that his hands are trembling. He dials Allie Read's number, then hurries to his window and peers across the street to see whether her lights are on. They are. He holds his breath until she answers the call.

Back on Aiken Avenue, in the fourth Row House from the left, Ruby Northrop runs upstairs after finishing an afternoon of work as the Doer of Unpleasant

Jobs. She has two bills in her pocket, and she fingers them eagerly. She closes her door, crosses the room to her desk, removes the envelope full of money, adds the bills to it, and begins counting. When she finishes, she lets out a sigh. At last she has enough to buy the owl.

Ruby hears her sister's footsteps on the stairs. A moment later, there's a knock on her door. "Can I come in?" calls Flora.

"No," Ruby says, and begins counting the money again.